T0285243

A VIEW FROM THE STARS

ALSO BY CIXIN LIU

A VIEW FROM THE STARS

CIXIN LIU

TRANSLATED BY

ANDY DUDAK   ADAM LANPHIER
JESSE FIELD   S. QIOUYI LU
ELIZABETH HANLON   HENRY ZHANG
EMILY XUENI JIN

TOR PUBLISHING GROUP
NEW YORK

A VIEW FROM THE STARS

Copyright © 2024 by 刘慈欣 (Cixin Liu)

English translation © 2024 by FT Culture (Beijing) Co., Ltd.

A Tor Book
Published by Tom Doherty Associates / Tor Publishing Group
120 Broadway
New York, NY 10271

www.tor-forge.com

Tor® is a registered trademark of Macmillan Publishing Group, LLC.

The Library of Congress Cataloging-in-Publication Data is available upon request.

ISBN 978-1-250-29211-7 (hardcover)
ISBN 978-1-250-35846-2 (international,
sold outside the U.S., subject to rights availability)
ISBN 978-1-250-29212-4 (ebook)

Our books may be purchased in bulk for promotional, educational, or business use. Please contact your local bookseller or the Macmillan Corporate and Premium Sales Department at 1-800-221-7945, extension 5442, or by email at MacmillanSpecialMarkets@macmillan.com.

First U.S. Edition: 2024
First International Edition: 2024

Printed in the United States of America

0 9 8 7 6 5 4 3 2 1

COPYRIGHT ACKNOWLEDGMENTS

CONTENTS

A VIEW FROM THE STARS

TIME ENOUGH FOR LOVE

TRANSLATED BY ADAM LANPHIER

Written September 21, 2015, in Yangquan, Shanxi
First published by Sichuan Science and Technology Press in January
2016 as a preface to *The Worst of All Possible Universes and the Best
of All Possible Earths: Liu Cixin's Sci-Fi Reviews and Essays*

It was a sweltering evening more than forty years ago. My family and I lived in a bungalow without electric fans, and it would be more than ten years before anyone had an air conditioner or television set—those may as well have been sci-fi technology. The adults were all outside, fanning themselves and chatting; I was alone in the house, sweating and reading. The book was the first work of sci-fi I'd ever read: Jules Verne's *Journey to the Center of the Earth*. My rapture was interrupted when someone snatched the book from my hands. It was my father. I was a bit nervous, because a few days before that he'd caught me reading *Red Crag*. He had scolded me and confiscated the book. (It's hard for people to imagine today, but back then, even red, revolutionary literature like *Red Crag* and *Song of Youth* was forbidden.) This time, however, my father said nothing. He just silently handed the book back to me. As I was impatiently preparing to reenter Verne's world, my father, who, last I'd checked, had been leaving the room, stopped at the door, turned his head, and said, "It's called science fiction."

That was the first time I heard the term that would shape my life. (It would be ten years before the abbreviation "sci-fi" appeared.) I can clearly recall my surprise—I'd thought it was a true story! Verne's writing was so realistic, and a significant portion of the many editions of *Journey to the Center of the Earth* that were published in China before the Cultural Revolution weren't labeled as science fiction on the cover, including the copy I was reading.

"This is all fantasy?" I asked.

"Yes, but it's based in science."

That simple, three-line exchange established the core concept that would later guide me as a writer of sci-fi.

I've previously named 1999, the year I had my first work published, as the year I began writing sci-fi. In truth, my creative journey began two decades before that. I wrote my first work of sci-fi in 1978. It was a short story about aliens visiting Earth. At the end, the aliens give the main character a gift: a little, squishy blob of some sort of membrane, small enough to hold in one hand. They tell him it's a balloon. He takes it home and blows it up, first with his mouth, then with a bicycle pump, then with a high-powered blower, and it expands into an enormous city, bigger than Beijing. I sent the manuscript to *New Port*, a literary publication based in Tianjin, and I may as well have thrown it into the old port, as I never heard back.

I wrote intermittently in the twenty years before "Whale Song" was published, with long breaks between my active periods. The traditional conception of sci-fi, as embodied in that three-line conversation with my father, had come under scrutiny as early as the beginning of the eighties and then was abandoned soon thereafter. The following decade, especially, saw a huge influx of new ideas, and Chinese sci-fi soaked them up like a sponge. And yet I felt as if I were standing solitary guard over a forlorn frontier, wandering in an empty wilderness, happening occasionally upon an overgrown ruin. To this day, that feeling of isolation is fresh in my mind. When things got hardest, I started to think strategically about my work. I wrote *China 2185* and *Supernova Era* hoping I could win publication with these, but deep down, I was still standing guard over that frontier. I subsequently gave up on long-form novels, returning instead to short stories and my own notion of what science fiction should be.

After I began publishing my work in *Science Fiction World*, I was delighted to discover that the frontier wasn't as barren as I'd thought. There were other people there, too, and the only reason we hadn't encountered each other was that I hadn't been perseverant enough in calling out to them. I went on to discover that there were no small number of people there. They appeared in droves, and, as I came to learn, they weren't only in China, but were in the US, too—a legion that together holds up a piece of sci-fi's sky, and held up my writing for the fifteen years that followed.

Sci-fi literature occupies an unusual position in China. As a genre, it is, by far, the subject of more theoretical thought, the target of deeper research and analysis, and the bearer of more new ideas and concepts than any other form of literature. Some topics have remained under debate for thirty or forty years, while new topics and issues constantly emerge and are subjected to research and discussion. No one cares more about theories and ideas than we do, and no one is more afraid of falling behind the vanguard of the times. And something strange has happened as a result.

In the month since I won the Hugo Award, I've had chances to talk sci-fi with people from all walks of life: the vice president of China, the mayor of my city, high school teachers, my daughter's classmates, traffic police, delivery boys, my neighborhood butcher with his pig heads . . . and in doing so, I've come to feel this strange thing more keenly.

What we in the community and in academia mean when we say "sci-fi" and what laypeople mean when they say it are more or less two different things.

On the one side, there are the hundreds of us in the sci-fi community; on the other, there are the pig head sellers, delivery boys, traffic police, daughters' classmates, high school teachers, mayors, and vice presidents, who number roughly 1.3 billion. Which side is wrong? I'll be honest—I really don't think it's us, though faced with such numbers, it's hard to say so with much confidence.

A famous author once said that classic literature, as represented by Tolstoy and Balzac, is a wall, built brick by brick, while modern and postmodern literature are a ladder that goes straight to the top.

This aptly describes the mindset of the sci-fi community, as well. We're always thinking about how to vault over the last thing, such that we forget that some things can't be skipped. They must be experienced. Our childhoods and youths, for instance—it's impossible to skip these parts of our lives and go straight to adulthood. As for sci-fi literature, we need that wall of bricks; without it, we'll have nowhere to prop up our ladders.

This collection* contains most of my nonfiction essays from the latter fifteen of my thirty-odd years as a writer of sci-fi. I wrote no essays about the genre in the twenty years before that, and there's not even a passing mention of it in my diaries from that time.

A trajectory emerges from these essays, taken together—a shift from paranoia to tolerance, from fanaticism to sobriety. I came to realize that

....

* *The Worst of All Possible Universes and the Best of All Possible Earths: Liu Cixin's Sci-Fi Reviews and Essays*

there are many kinds of sci-fi, and I learned that a work of sci-fi might contain no science. Sci-fi can turn its gaze from outer space and the future toward mundane reality; it can even focus solely on one's own interior life. Each kind of sci-fi exists for a reason, and a classic of the genre might come from any of them.

Even so, the concept underlying that short exchange with my father is a boulder in my heart. I still believe it to be the basis for sci-fi literature's existence. This, too, is what all these essays are trying to express.

Though it's been afoot for a hundred years, Chinese science fiction is just getting started. The years ahead beckon to us. There's time enough for love.

WHALE SONG

TRANSLATED BY S. QIOUYI LU

Written January 1999, at Niangzi Pass
First published in *Science Fiction World*, 1999, no. 6

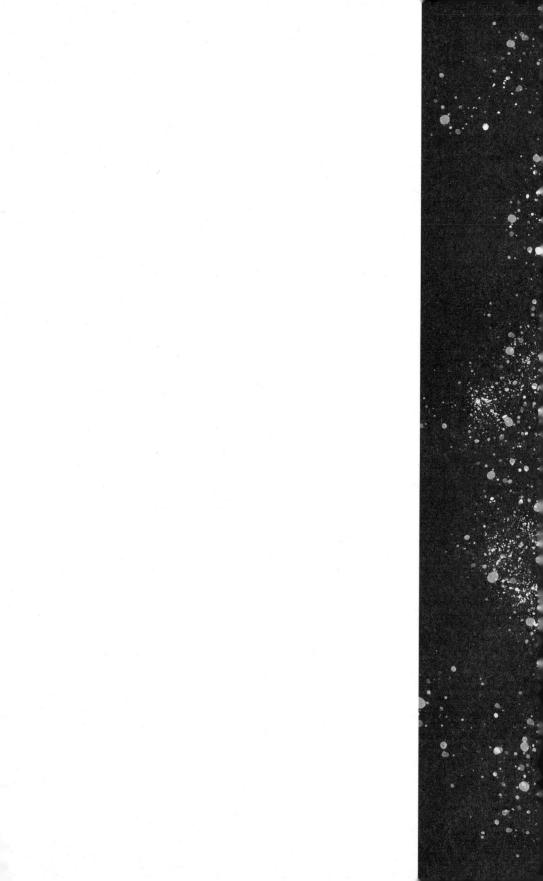

Uncle Warner stood at the bow of the boat contemplating the Atlantic Ocean's tranquil surface. He rarely contemplated things, eschewing elaborate forethought in favor of following his instinct.

But now, the game had changed.

Uncle Warner wasn't the demon that the media made him out to be. In fact, he looked like Santa Claus. Incisive gaze aside, he always had a bold yet sweet smile on his face. He was never armed, except for the exquisite knife he carried in his breast pocket, which he used to peel fruit and to kill people.

He smiled doing both.

In addition to the eighty subordinates and two South American girls aboard, Uncle Warner also had twenty-five tons of pure heroin stashed in his three-thousand-ton megayacht—two years' worth of product from his refinery deep in the jungles of South America. A couple of months ago, the National Army of Colombia had surrounded the refinery to seize the shipment. His younger brother and more than thirty of his subordinates died in the struggle.

He badly needed the money he'd get from this shipment to construct a new refinery, perhaps in Bolivia this time, or even in Southeast Asia's Golden Triangle. He had to ensure the continued survival of the drug empire he'd worked so hard to build. But even after floating on the sea for a month, he still hadn't gotten a single gram of product onto US shores. Going through customs was completely out of the question. The instant a neutrino detector goes off, it becomes impossible to keep drugs hidden. A year ago, they tried casting heroin into the cores of steel bars to be imported, but they'd been found out all too easily.

Then, Uncle Warner thought up an ingenious plan: They'd load about 50 kg of product onto a light aircraft, usually a cheap Cessna, and fly in via Miami. Once they reached the shore, the pilot would strap the product onto their body and jump out with a parachute. Although it was a waste of an aircraft, the 50 kg of product still fetched a hefty profit. It was an invincible strategy for a while, but then the Americans used satellites and land-based radar to construct an aerial surveillance system capable of discovering and even tracking the parachuting pilots. Before Uncle Warner's brave lads could take the plunge, they'd find police already waiting for them on the ground.

Uncle Warner then attempted to use small boats to get product ashore, but the results were even more disastrous. The Coast Guard's speedboats had all been outfitted with neutrino detectors. As soon as one of Uncle Warner's boats came within three thousand meters of the patrol, a scan instantly revealed the drugs on board. Uncle Warner even considered using mini submarines, but the Americans had long since perfected their underwater monitoring network, first created during the Cold War. The submarine would be detected long before it reached the shore.

Uncle Warner was at his wits' end. He hated scientists—they were the ones who'd caused all this. Then again, scientists could also be of service to him here. He put his American-educated son to work on that front. Money wasn't an issue.

That morning, Warner Jr. disembarked from another boat and boarded the yacht, telling his father that he had found the person they were looking for.

"He's a genius, Dad. I met him at Caltech."

Warner Sr. wrinkled his nose disdainfully. "Hmph. You've wasted three years at Caltech and you're still no genius. Are they really that easy to come by?"

"He really *is* a genius, Dad!"

Warner Sr. turned and sat on a chair laid out on the forward deck. He took out his exquisite knife and began peeling a pineapple. The two South American girls stepped over to rub his meaty shoulders. The person Warner Jr. brought had kept far off to one side, looking out toward the ocean, but he came over now. He was shockingly thin. His neck was like a dowel—it was hard to believe that it could prop up such an unsurpassably huge head, rendering his appearance uncanny.

"This is Dave Hopkins. He holds a Ph.D. in marine biology," Warner Jr. said, introducing the man.

"I heard you can help us out, sir." Warner Sr. smiled his Santa smile.

"Yes, I can help you get the shipment ashore," Hopkins said, expressionless.

"Using what?"

"Whales."

Warner Jr. gestured for a couple of his people to carry over a strange object. It was a submersible made of some kind of clear plastic. A meter tall and two meters long, the submersible's streamlined cabin was about the same size as a small car's. There were two seats, a simple dashboard with a small screen, and a designated space behind the seats, clearly intended for storing the product.

"This submersible can carry two people and about a ton of product," Hopkins said.

"And how is this thing supposed to go five hundred kilometers underwater to get to Miami's shore?"

"In a whale's mouth."

Warner Sr. guffawed, the sound sharp at first before growing coarse. He used that laugh to express everything: amusement, fury, doubt, despair, fear, grief . . . every time he laughed, only he knew why.

"Clever kid! So how much do I have to pay the fish for it to take us to our destination?"

"Whales aren't fish. They're marine mammals with blowholes. You can give the money to me. I've already installed a bioorganic device in its brain, along with a computer that can receive incoming signals and convert them into the whale's brainwaves. You can control the whale's behavior with this."

Hopkins retrieved a device from his pocket that resembled a television remote control.

Warner Sr.'s laughter became even more uproarious.

"Hahaha . . . This kid must've seen *Pinocchio*, haha . . . Ahaha . . ." He bent over double, wheezing, the pineapple in his hand tumbling to the ground. "Haha . . . that puppet, ah, Pinocchio—with an old man, too, swallowed into the belly of a fish . . . haha . . ."

"Dad, just listen, his plan could really work!" Warner Jr. pleaded.

". . . Ahahaha . . . Pinocchio and the old man were in that fish's belly for a while. Maybe they're still in there! Hahaha . . . still lighting candles . . . hahahaha . . ."

Warner Sr. stopped laughing then, his wild guffawing ceasing abruptly like a light going out, though his Santa smile remained. He asked one of the girls behind him, "What happens when Pinocchio lies?"

"His nose grows," the girl replied.

Warner Sr. stood, the knife he'd used to peel the pineapple in one hand, his other hand on Hopkins's chin, tilting his face up so he could observe his nose as the girls behind him watched mildly.

"Is his nose getting longer?" he asked the girls with a smile.

"It is, Uncle Warner!" the girls said in saccharine unison, as if seeing people meet their demise at his hands was a pleasure of theirs.

"Then let's help him out," Warner Sr. said. His son wasn't quick enough to stop him. Warner Sr.'s quick knife sliced off the tip of Hopkins's nose. Blood gushed from the wound, but Hopkins was still as tranquil as ever. Even after Warner Sr. released his hold on Hopkins's chin, Hopkins continued to stand there with his arms hanging by his sides, letting the blood flow freely, as if his nose weren't even part of his face.

"Put this genius in that contraption and throw him into the ocean." Warner Sr. waved a hand. The two girls shoved Hopkins into the clear submersible. Then, Warner Sr. picked up the remote and handed it to Hopkins through the door, as amiably as if he were Santa Claus handing a gift to a child.

"Take it. Summon your precious fish. Hahaha . . ."

He guffawed again. But as soon as the submersible hit the water with a huge splash, his smile disappeared, revealing a rare moment of solemnity.

"He'll die there sooner or later," he said to his son.

The submersible sank into the ocean waves, as weak and helpless as a bubble.

Suddenly, the two girls screamed. A massive swell of water surged forth about two hundred meters away from the yacht. It moved astonishingly fast, soon splitting into two great waves as a black ridge broke the surface.

"It's a whale. Forty-eight meters long. Hopkins calls it Poseidon, after the Greek god of the ocean," Warner Jr. said into his father's ear.

The ridge disappeared a dozen meters away from the submersible, its colossal fluke waving in its wake like a black sail. Then, the whale's enormous head appeared beside the submersible. It opened its massive maw and swallowed the submersible in one gulp, as if it were an ordinary fish eating bread crumbs. After that, the whale came back around to the megayacht. The living mountain approached solemnly, bombarding the yacht with breaking waves as it boomed out a rumbling call. Even a person as arrogant as Warner Sr. could be awed by such a sight. He was witnessing a god: an embodiment of the ocean's might, an incarnation of nature's power.

The whale completed its circle around the yacht. Then, it turned and stormed the ship, its massive head breaking the water's surface right beside it. The people aboard could clearly see the barnacles clinging to the whale's coarse, pebbled skin. It was only then that they truly realized how huge the whale was.

The whale opened its jaws and spit out the tiny submersible. The submersible arced over the side of the yacht in nearly a straight line before clattering onto the deck. The door opened. Hopkins emerged, the front of his shirt wet with blood from his nose, but he was otherwise unscathed.

"Hurry and call the doctor! Can't you see that Pinocchio's injured?!" Warner Sr. bellowed, as if Hopkins's injury had nothing to do with him.

"My name is Dave Hopkins," Hopkins said severely.

"I'm calling you Pinocchio," Warner said, once again donning his Santa Claus smile.

A few hours later, Warner and Hopkins wormed into the submersible, placing the ton of heroin wrapped in a waterproof bag behind the seats. Warner had decided to go himself. He needed to take risks to invigorate the sluggish blood in his veins, and this would be, without a doubt, the most invigorating trip he'd ever had. The sailors on the yacht lowered the submersible with thick cables to the ocean's surface, then cruised away.

Waves jolted the two passengers. The submersible bobbed on the water's surface, illuminated by the setting sun. Hopkins pressed a button on the remote to summon the whale. There was a low, muffled sound of something stirring far off in distant waters. The sound grew louder and louder until the whale's maw broke through the surface. It pressed on toward them, then sucked the submersible into a black abyss. The light retreated, narrowing into a thin gap before going out completely, plunging them into the dark. There was a loud *chomp*: the sound of the whale's titanic teeth crashing shut. Then, a zero-gravity feeling like plummeting in an elevator. The whale was diving into deeper, stealthier waters.

"How clever, Pinocchio! Hahaha . . ." Warner broke out into raucous laughter again in the dark, either expressing or masking his terror.

"Let's light some candles, sir," Hopkins said, his voice happy and at ease. This was his domain. When Warner realized that, his terror deepened. A ceiling light came on in the cabin, bathing them in a dim ultramarine light.

The first thing Warner saw outside the submersible was a row of white pillars, each as tall as a person and tapered to a sharp point. The upper and lower pillars interlocked into a row of bars. He quickly realized that he was looking at the whale's teeth. The submersible seemed to be resting on a soft, wriggling mire. Above them was a vaulted ceiling supported by row after row of arched bone. The mire and roof beams all tilted toward an enormous black hole that kept changing shape. Warner's manic laughter started up again. The hole led to the whale's throat. Shrouded in a wet haze under the blue light's glow, the two of them seemed to be in a mythical grotto.

The display in the submersible showed a nautical chart of the Bahamas and the area around Miami. Hopkins used the remote to "drive" the whale. A line tracing the ship's path appeared, mapping out a route to Warner's destination on Miami's shores.

"We've embarked on our journey. Poseidon is fast. We should arrive in about five hours," Hopkins said.

"Won't we suffocate?" Warner asked, doing his best to hide his anxiety.

"Of course not. I told you, whales have blowholes. They breathe oxygen, too. We've got more than enough around us. Once it's been filtered, we can breathe like we normally do."

"Pinocchio, you truly are the Devil! How did you come up with all this? For a start, how did you insert the controls and computer into this big fella's brain?"

"One person can't do it alone. To begin, the animal needs to be sedated with a five-hundred-kilogram dose of anesthesia. Poseidon is property of the US Navy; I oversaw the multibillion-dollar military research project that he was part of. He was used during the Cold War to transport spies and special forces to the shores of the Warsaw Pact countries. I oversaw other projects as well, such as implanting devices into the brains of dolphins and sharks so that they could be strapped with explosives and used as torpedoes. I did so much for my country, but, as soon as there were budget cuts, they kicked me to the curb. As I left the research lab, I took Poseidon with me. These past few years, we've swum the seven seas together . . ."

"Then Pinocchio, do you have any, hmm, ethical qualms about using your Poseidon for these kinds of activities? Of course, I'm sure me talking about ethics is laughable to you, but I had chemists and engineers working for me in my refinery who often had those kinds of misgivings."

"I have no such thing, sir. Humanity recruiting innocent creatures into their vile wars is already the greatest sin. I devoted myself to my country and its military; I had the qualifications to get what I wanted. And since society denied me that, I might as well go take it myself."

"Hahahaha . . . Yes, best to take it yourself! Hahaha . . ." Warner laughed, then stopped suddenly. "Listen—what's that sound?"

"It's the sound of Poseidon spouting water. He's breathing. The submersible is fitted with a sensitive sonar that can amplify the sounds outside. Listen . . ."

A droning sound mixed with the crashing of the waves, going from soft to loud, then loud to soft again, until it gradually faded out.

"It's a ten-thousand-ton oil tanker."

Before them, the two rows of teeth yawned open. Seawater boomed as it surged in, drowning the submersible. Hopkins pressed a button. The nautical charts on the screen disappeared, replaced by a complicated waveform: Poseidon's brainwaves.

"Oh! Poseidon's discovered a school of fish. It's lunchtime."

The whale bared its gullet, revealing the pitch-black of a deep ocean abyss. A school of fish surfaced and streamed into Poseidon's maw, banging against the submersible as they flooded past, dazzling and flashing silver in the submersible's light. Believing that they were swimming into a cave full of coral, the fish were unaware of their fate.

A crash pulsed through the flurry of fish. Barely visible beyond the wall of teeth coming together were the whale's still-parted lips. A howling torrent of water tumbled the fish backward until they were plastered against the pillars of teeth. The whale was expelling the seawater in its mouth, and the great pressure was also filtering out the tide that had come in with the school of fish. Astonished, Warner watched as water surged perpendicularly past the submersible. The whale soon emptied out the rest of the water, leaving the fish flopping wildly against each other in front of the pillars of teeth. The soft "ground" beneath the submersible began to squirm, turning into a great, undulating wave that coaxed the fish backward. By the time Warner realized what was happening, terror had gripped him from head to toe.

"Don't worry. Poseidon won't swallow us," Hopkins said, understanding the reason for Warner's terror. "It can filter us out, just as we can separate the shell from the kernel while eating sunflower seeds. The submersible affects its eating, but it's used to it. Sometimes, when there's a large school of fish, it'll temporarily spit out the submersible before eating."

Warner let out a relieved sigh. He wanted to laugh again, but he didn't have the strength to. He stared, dumbstruck, as the fish flopped past the absolutely stationary submersible to the black abyss behind them. Once the two or three tons of fish disappeared into the whale's gullet, there was a boom like a landslide.

The shock sank Warner into a long silence. Hopkins nudged him: "Did you hear that?" As he spoke, he turned up the volume on the sonar's loudspeaker.

Warner heard a low rumble. Confused, he looked at Hopkins.

"Poseidon is singing. It's a whale song."

Gradually, Warner picked a rhythm and even a melody out of the low, intermittent call. "What is it doing? Looking for a mate?"

"Not entirely. Marine biologists have been researching the topic for a long time, but even now, the meaning of whale song isn't entirely clear."

"Maybe it's meaningless."

"Precisely the opposite. The meaning is too deep for humans to understand. Researchers believe it's a kind of musical language, but one that can express far more than any human language."

Whale song is the soul of the ocean singing. In whale song, ancient lightning strikes the primordial sea, life glimmering in the chaos of the ocean; in whale song, life opens its curious and awestruck eyes, stepping out of the sea for the first time on scaled feet onto continents still alive with volcanoes; in whale song, a dinosaur empire goes extinct in a flash of cold—time slips by, and a world of changes passes in an instant, wisdom like blades of grass sprouting in the warmth left after a glacier's passage; in whale song, civilization rises like a specter on every continent, and Atlantis crumbles into the sea in a grand cataclysm . . . Naval war after naval war stains the ocean red with blood; countless empires rise and fall, each a wisp of smoke passing before one's eyes . . .

The whale drew from its ancient, unfathomable memory to sing the song of life, completely unaware of the tiny, insignificant evil in its mouth.

The whale reached Miami at midnight, stopping a couple of hundred meters from the shore so it wouldn't run aground. Everything went surprisingly smoothly. The moonlight that evening was good; Warner and Hopkins could clearly see the groves of palm trees on the shore and the eight runners wearing wetsuits waiting for them. They swiftly moved the ton of product ashore and readily paid the highest price Warner asked, even promising to buy however much product they had in the future. They were amazed that the little clear submersible could get past the strictly enforced maritime defense line; at first, they hadn't been sure if Warner and Hopkins were people or ghosts (Hopkins had already instructed Poseidon to swim far away).

Half an hour later, with the runners long gone, Hopkins once again summoned Poseidon. He hauled two briefcases of American bills as he and Warner boarded for their return journey.

"Excellent, Pinocchio!" Warner cheered. "Today's profits are all yours. We'll split future profits. You're rich, Pinocchio! Hahaha . . . We'll still have to make another twenty-something runs to distribute the rest of the twenty-something tons."

"We might not need to make that many trips. With a few changes, I think we can transport two or three tons at a time."

"Hahahaha . . . Outstanding, Pinocchio!"

During the tranquil underwater journey, Warner fell asleep. After some time, Hopkins woke him. He glanced at the map and route on the small screen and realized that they'd already traveled two-thirds of their journey. Nothing seemed out of the ordinary.

"Listen."

He heard a ferry on the surface. They had been a common sight on the last journey. Uncomprehending, he looked at Hopkins. But as he kept listening, he realized that the ferry didn't sound right. It was different from before. This time, the volume didn't change.

The boat was following the whale.

"How long has it been following us?" Warner asked.

"About half an hour. I've changed our route several times."

"How can this be? The Coast Guard's patrol boat wouldn't detect a whale on a scan."

"So what if they do a scan? The whale's not carrying any drugs right now."

"Plus, if they wanted to take care of us, it would've been easier to do so in Miami. Why wait until now?" Baffled, Warner peered at the nautical map on the screen. They'd already passed through the Straits of Florida and were headed toward Cuba.

"Poseidon has to breathe. We have no choice but to surface—just a few seconds should be enough." Hopkins picked up the remote. Warner nodded; Hopkins pressed the remote. A weight settled on them as the whale ascended. With a breaking wave, the whale surfaced.

The sonar made a sudden, muffled sound. The submersible shuddered. The sonar sounded again; the whale thrashed more wildly, tumbling the submersible around its mouth. The submersible slammed heavily into the whale's teeth a few times, landing with a *crack* that nearly knocked Warner and Hopkins unconscious.

"The ship's started firing at us!" Hopkins yelled in surprise. He did his best to calm the whale with the remote and send neural instructions, but the whale ignored the commands as it continued its aimless thrashing on the ocean's surface.

The whale's massive body was trembling—a tremble of pain.

"We have to get out, or else!" Warner shouted.

Hopkins issued the command to eject the submersible. This time, the whale obeyed. With shocking speed, the submersible burst out of its mouth and plunked onto the surface. The sun had already risen over the Atlantic, making them squint. But they quickly realized that they were sitting in water. The battering they'd taken in the whale's mouth had cracked the hull, and seawater was flooding in. The entire submersible was mangled; even with all their strength, they couldn't pull open the hatch to escape. They started to use whatever they could to plug up the holes, even using bundles of bills from the briefcases, but it was no use—the seawater continued to surge in, and soon, the water in the submersible was chest-deep.

Before the submersible sank, Hopkins saw the other boat. It was huge and had a strangely shaped cannon at its bow. With a flash, the cannon fired a harpoon into the struggling whale's back.

The whale beat against the waves with the last of its strength. Its blood had already stained the water red.

The submersible sank into the infinite billows of the whale's crimson blood.

"Who's responsible for our death?" Warner asked, the water up to his chin.

"The whaler," Hopkins replied.

Warner guffawed for the last time.

"The international pledge completely banned whaling five years ago! These sons of bitches!" Hopkins said, letting loose a stream of obscenities.

Warner continued laughing. "Hahaha . . . they're unscrupulous . . . hahahaha . . . society won't give it to them . . . hahaha . . . they'll get it themselves . . . haha . . . get it themselves . . ."

As the seawater filled the submersible, in their last moments of consciousness, Hopkins and Warner heard Poseidon sing its solemn whale song again. Life's last song carried through the bloody Atlantic, echoing, echoing, everlasting.

A JOURNEY IN SEARCH OF HOME

On the Inclusion of "The Wandering Earth" in the 30th Anniversary of *Science Fiction World*

TRANSLATED BY HENRY ZHANG

Written August 2009, at Niangzi Pass
First published in *Science Fiction World: The 30th Anniversary Supplement* in September 2009

I wrote "The Wandering Earth" for the 1999 *Science Fiction World* writ-ers' conference. At the time, the editor asked all of us to bring our own work; in addition to this story, I took along "Whale Song," "At the End of the Microcosmos," and "Time Migration" (all unpublished then). It was the first time I'd engaged with the science fiction community.

I remember it was already very late when I got to the Sichuan As-sociation for Science & Technology Guesthouse, located next to the magazine's editorial office. In front of the reception desk, I saw a young man and woman, he more handsome and she more beautiful than any-one I'd seen before, like figures from a myth. I immediately decided that they must be science fiction writers, here to attend the conference—unconsciously, I believed that science fiction was as beautiful as they were. So, I hurried up to them and asked whether they were here to attend the convention, and they laughed and said they weren't (they were probably students traveling during break). Only on the second morning, when the writers and editors began to appear in the lobby of the hostel, did I realize I wasn't looking at gods, but mortals like me—that myths were written by people who didn't belong in them, that the pair of beautiful young people I'd seen the previous night were no more capable of writing myths or science fiction than we are of pulling our-selves up by the hair.

At that particular conference, Alai invited Feng Min, senior editor at *Journal of Short Stories*, to give a lecture on the state of mainstream Chinese literature, and emphasized the need for science fiction novels to find a balance between a literary and a scientific imaginary. In fact, "The Wandering Earth" is a product of this balancing act.

From both a scientific and a sci-fi perspective, if humanity had to engage in mass exodus, as is the case in my short story, I would cast my vote with the faction that wanted to escape in spaceships. An over-whelming majority of the energy needed to propel Earth would be wasted on useless structural load: the matter of the planet's crust. Such matter gives us gravity, but gravity can also be simulated by rotating the spaceships that carry us. Yet from a literary point of view, the story's aesthetic core is the motif that science can push the entire planet through its itinerary among the stars. Using spaceships to flee makes much less of an aesthetic impact.

Later, though, something happened to me that almost resulted in the story's stillbirth. During a work trip, I rode a plane for the first time. As I looked at Earth from several miles high, I still wasn't able to perceive its curvature; the planet's surface still appeared as an endless plane—it was a fool's dream to move such a planet! But after returning home, I persisted in finishing. The first version was only half as long as the published one, but upon my editor's suggestion, I doubled the length. When I read the story at the convention, Wang Jinkang commented that only a story of three hundred thousand characters could have fleshed out my idea. But I didn't have the chance to turn it into a novel then.

In writing "The Wandering Earth," I was forced to sacrifice scientific rigor in many parts. For example, helium flashes are phenomena that occur only in the latter part of a star's life; only after they occur repeatedly and across a huge span of time can a star become a red giant. Apart from this, my inexperience prompted me to write out the exact specifications of the Earth's propulsion engines, so that it would be easy to calculate the amount of acceleration they provided Earth. When calculated, these numbers would have resulted in engines that barely increased the Earth's acceleration. They wouldn't even be able to shift its orbit, let alone propel it through space.

Over the years, I've heard and read a lot of feedback on my work. Some people blabber on for ages and I don't understand them, but some can use a single sentence to reveal truths that were hidden from me. During a conference in 2000, Yang Ping told me he thought he sensed a strong "longing for home" in my novels. At the time I didn't agree; I believed such a longing was antithetical to my writing. But now I have to shake my head in admiration, and admit he got it right. Ten years later, a lot has changed, and very soon, I'm going to leave the place I've lived for more than two decades. It was here that I spent most of my youth, and where I wrote all of my science fiction, but now that it's time to leave, I find I'm not reluctant at all. This isn't my home, spiritually—I don't know where that home is. Now, as I look at the mountain range outside my window, Ping's words ring in my head again. In fact, my journey in science fiction really has taken me on the path toward home. Such a yearning lurked so deep inside of me that I didn't know it, because I didn't know where home was. That was why I had to go so far to look for it. "The Wandering Earth" stages exactly this kind of scene: a traveler, setting out on a long journey, accompanied by loneliness and terror.

THE
MESSENGER

TRANSLATED BY ANDY DUDAK

Written January 2001, at Niangzi Pass
First published in *King of Science Fiction*, 2001, no. 11

The old man had only yesterday noticed the listener downstairs. His spirits were quite low these days, and except for when he played his violin, he didn't look out the window much. He meant to isolate himself from the outside world with the window curtain, and with his music, but it was impossible.

Many years ago, over on the other side of the Atlantic, when he rocked a baby pram in a narrow garret and flipped through uninteresting patent applications in a bustling patent office, his ideas were still immersed in a beautiful world. In that world, he ran at the speed of light. Now he was in the quiet, secluded little town of Princeton. The detachment of his youth was gone. The outside world was constantly perplexing and disturbing.

Two matters in particular troubled him. One was quantum theory, originated by Max Planck and now the obsession of so many young physicists. It made him uneasy, particularly the theory's indeterminacy. "God doesn't play dice," he often said to himself these days. He had, in the latter half of his life, devoted himself to concocting a unified field theory, but had made no progress. What he'd built was pure math and no physics. The other matter that troubled him was the atom bomb. It had been a long time since Hiroshima and Nagasaki, a long time since the war, but his pain, which had been a dull wound, had now flared with agony. Such a small, simple formula. All it did was relate mass to energy. Truth be told, before Fermi's reactor pile was built, the old man thought humans turning mass into energy at the atomic level was a wild fantasy. Helen Dukas had been consoling him a lot lately. But she didn't realize he was unconcerned with his own merits, errors, honor, or disgrace—his worries were more far-reaching.

In recent dreams, he kept hearing a fearful sort of din, like a deluge or a volcano. Finally, one night, the clamor woke him and he discovered it was only a small puppy snoring on the patio. The noise never invaded his dreams again. He dreamt of a wasteland, the setting sun reflected on melting snow. He tried to escape this wasteland, but it was too big, seemingly limitless. Later he saw an ocean, the setting sun again, the sea bloodred, and he understood. The whole world was a wasteland covered in melting snow. He woke with a start once more. This time, a question emerged in his mind like a dark reef at ebb tide:

Does humanity still have a future?

The question tormented him like a raging fire, nearly intolerable.

The person downstairs was young. He wore a stylish nylon jacket. The old man realized this visitor was listening to his violin. For the next three days, whenever the old man began his evening playing, the visitor would arrive and stand quietly in the fading glow of the Princeton sunset. Around nine o'clock the old man would put down his violin, and the listener would slowly depart. Maybe he was a Princeton University student, or just someone who'd heard the old man lecture. The old man had long ago grown weary of his countless worshippers, the sycophants of every kind, from kings to housewives. But this stranger downstairs, this friend so interested in his musical talent, this one gave him a kind of consolation. On the fourth night, the old man had just begun to play when it started raining. He looked out the window and saw the young man standing under the only available shelter: a Chinese parasol tree. The rain worsened, and the tree's sparse autumnal foliage provided little cover. The old man stopped playing, wishing to release his audience early. But the young man seemed to know this wasn't the concert's proper ending time. He remained standing there, unmoving, his saturated jacket shining under the streetlamp. The old man put down his violin. He went unsteadily down the stairs and out into the misty rain, and finally he was standing before the young visitor.

"If you . . . eh, would like to listen, why not come upstairs?"

Not waiting for an answer, the old man turned and went back inside. The visitor stood there staring, as if into limitless distance, as if what just happened had been a dream. The music resumed upstairs. The visitor entered the front door in a kind of trance. He went upstairs, as if drawn by the spirit of the music. The old man's door was half open. The visitor went inside. The old man faced the window and watched the rain as he played. He didn't turn his head, but he sensed the young man had arrived. He felt a bit apologetic toward his audience, this person so infatuated with his violin's voice. He didn't play particularly well. Today's selection in particular, his favorite Mozart rondo, he often played out of tune. Sometimes he forgot a phrase and used his imagination to fill the gap. He still had this cheap violin, his old friend, its voice far from precise. But the young listener seemed calm and content. The two of them were soon immersed in the instrument's flawed but imaginative sound.

This was an unremarkable night in the mid-twentieth century. The Iron Curtain separated East from West. Humanity's future, recently fallen under the nuclear shadow, was like the dim, misty, rainy autumn evening. On this night, in the rain, Mozart's rondo floated out of this little house in Princeton, New Jersey.

Time seemed to pass faster than usual. Nine o'clock rolled around soon enough. The old man stopped playing and looked up to see his guest bow, then turn to go.

"Eh, will you come and listen tomorrow?" the old man asked.

The young man stood at the door and didn't turn around. "I'm afraid not, Professor. Tomorrow you will have a visitor." He opened the door, then seemed to recall something. "Oh, that's right. Your guest will leave at 8:10. Will you still play afterward?"

The old man nodded distractedly, not grasping the implication of these words.

"Very well then, I will come. Thank you."

The rain continued unabated the next day, and evening did indeed bring a guest, the Israeli ambassador. The old man had always given that remote, newborn country his blessing—they were his people over there, his tribe—and he'd donated the proceeds from selling his original manuscripts to the cause. But this time, the ambassador wanted something else. The old man didn't know whether to laugh or cry. They wanted him to be president of Israel! He firmly declined. He accompanied the ambassador back into the rain, and fished out his pocket watch just before the man got in his car. Under the streetlamp, the timepiece showed 8:10. A memory stirred.

"Your . . . eh, your visit . . . did anyone else know about it?"

"Rest assured, Professor. This is all a rigorously kept secret. Nobody knows."

Perhaps that young visitor knew, but somehow he also knew . . . The old man asked a very odd question: "So, had you planned on leaving at 8:10?"

"Pardon me? Well, no. I hoped to chat with you at length, but since you've refused, I've no wish to disturb you. We understand, Professor."

The old man returned upstairs, perplexed, but when he took out his little violin, he forgot his bewilderment. The music had just begun when the young man appeared.

Their concert ended at ten o'clock, and the old man repeated yesterday's invitation: "Will you come and listen tomorrow?" He thought a bit and added, "I think this is nice."

"Well, tomorrow I can listen from below again."

"But I think it will still be raining tomorrow. These are cloudy days."

"You're right, it will rain tomorrow, but not when it comes time for you to play. The next day, when you play again, I'll come up to listen. The rain won't stop until 11 A.M. the following morning."

The old man laughed, thinking the young visitor very funny indeed, but watching him leave, he had a sudden premonition that none of this was a joke.

His premonition was correct. The weather over the next few days bore out the young man's predictions. On the rainless evening, he remained downstairs listening. It was raining at concert time the following day, and he came upstairs. It stopped raining in Princeton at precisely 11 A.M. the next morning.

The first clear night after the weather, the young visitor forwent listening downstairs and came up to the old man's room, bringing with him a small violin. Saying nothing, he presented it with both hands to the old man.

"No no, please. I have no use for another violin." The old man waved it away. Many people had offered him violins, among them famous and valuable Italian instruments, ones that had belonged to celebrated players—and he'd politely refused them one by one, feeling his skill did not merit such great violins.

"I'm lending this to you. After a while you'll return it to me. Sorry, Professor, you can't keep it."

The old man took it, and on close inspection it seemed a common sort of violin. It didn't seem to have strings, surprisingly, though a more careful look revealed that it did, but the strings were extremely fine, like spider threads. The old man didn't dare press down on them. The gossamer seemed a breath away from breaking. He looked up at the visitor, who smiled and nodded, so he lightly pressed the strings. They didn't snap, indeed they felt impossibly strong beneath his fingertips. He brought the bow to bear, inadvertently sliding it along one string and making it sound—and it was like hearing the cry of Nature itself.

It was the voice of the Sun, the Sun of all voices.

The old man launched upon the rondo, and right away he was one with the boundless cosmos. He saw light waves propagating through space, slowly, like mist blown by a morning breeze; undulating gravitational swells of the vast space-time membrane, and the countless stars floating on that membrane like sparkling dewdrops; a mighty gale of energy blowing across the membrane, conjuring dreamlike secondary rainbows.

When the old man woke from his musical reverie, the young visitor had gone.

The old man was fascinated with the violin. He played every day, and into the late hours of the night. Dukas and his doctor both urged him to consider his health, but they also knew that every time that violin music started, a vigor he'd never known would surge through his veins.

The young visitor had yet to return.

After ten days, he started playing the strange violin less, even sometimes going back to his original violin, that old friend. He'd started worrying that excessive use might wear down or even break the fine gossamer strings. But he couldn't resist the sounds that came out of that instrument. It was like he was enchanted. He began to think of the young visitor's return, whenever that might be, and having to give up the violin, and he resumed playing it all night long like he had at first. Every night, in the wee hours, when he reluctantly stopped playing, he would carefully examine the strings. His vision had gone dim with age, but he had Dukas find a magnifying glass, under which the strings showed no sign of wear or abrasion. Their surface was like precious stone, glossy, sparkling, translucent, in the dark, even fluorescing blue.

Another ten days passed.

It was late, and it had become his habit to gaze at the violin just before falling asleep. Something about the strings struck him as peculiar. He picked up the magnifying glass and examined the strings closely, confirming his suspicion. Actually, the inkling had begun several days before, but only now had the change become pronounced enough to easily perceive.

The strings were thickening with use.

The next night, when the old man had just put bow to string, the young visitor suddenly appeared.

"You've come for this, haven't you?" the old man asked uneasily.

The visitor nodded.

"Eh . . . perhaps you could let me have it?"

"Absolutely not. My apologies, Professor, but it's impossible. I can't leave anything behind now."

The old man thought about this and began to understand. He offered up the violin with both hands. "It's not from this time, is it?"

The young man shook his head, standing by the window. Outside, the Milky Way traversed the vast sky, the stars resplendent. He was a black silhouette before this magnificent backdrop.

The old man understood more. He recalled the visitor's mysterious predictive talents. It was quite simple really. He hadn't been predicting. He'd been remembering.

"I'm a messenger. In our time, we unexpectedly saw how worried you are, so I was dispatched."

"And you brought me what?" the old man said, unamazed. "This violin?" Throughout his life, the cosmos had been one big wonder to him. It was precisely because of this that he'd surpassed others and been the first to glimpse the universe's deepest mystery.

"No, the violin is just proof that I'm from the future."

"Proof?"

"In this era of yours, people convert mass into energy. You have the atom bomb and very soon you'll have the fusion bomb. In our era, we can turn energy into mass. You see . . ." He pointed at the violin strings. ". . . they're getting thicker. The increased mass is converted sonic energy, from when you play."

The old man shook his head in bafflement.

"I know these revelations go against your theory. Firstly, I can't possibly travel back in time. Secondly, according to your formula, it would take a huge amount of energy to increase the strings' mass as much as you have."

The old man was silent awhile. He smiled indulgently. "Eh . . . theory is ambiguous, gray." He sighed. "And the tree of my life has also turned gray. Okay, child, what have you brought for me?"

"Two pieces of news."

"And the first is?"

"Humanity has a future."

The old man sank into an armchair, relieved. He was like every old man who finally settles his life's ultimate and long-cherished wish. A sense of well-being suffused him from head to toe. He could really rest. "I suppose I should have known that, child, since you are here."

"The atom bombs used on Japan will be the last nuclear weapons used in combat. By the end of the 1990s, most countries will have signed an international agreement banning nuclear weapons testing and preventing proliferation. Fifty years after that, the last warhead will be destroyed. And I'll be born two hundred years after that."

The young man picked up the violin he meant to reclaim. "I should go. I've already delayed many journeys in order to hear your music. I still have three eras to visit, and five people to meet, among them the creator of the unified field theory. I'm afraid that's a matter for a century hence."

What he didn't mention was that he always chose a time near death to pay these formal visits to great people, to minimize affecting the future.

"And what is the second piece of news you have for me?"

The young man had opened the door. He turned, smiling apologetically.

"Professor, I'm afraid God does indeed play dice."

The old man watched through his window as the visitor left the house. It was quite late and the street was empty. The young man began to undress. It seemed he didn't want to bring this era's clothes with him. The skintight suit he wore underneath fluoresced in the dim light—his era's garb, obviously. He didn't exit by transforming into white light, as the old man had imagined. He rose into the air, rapidly, at an angle, and a few seconds later he vanished among the brilliant stars of the night sky. His speed had been constant—no acceleration. Clearly, he had not risen as such. Earth had revolved while he had remained static, at absolute rest in this space-time. The old man reckoned the messenger could use his absolute space-time coordinates as a starting point, like standing on the bank of the long river of space-time, and watch time surging by, and if he wanted, go anywhere he liked upriver or down.

Albert Einstein stood there for a while in silence, then slowly turned, and once more picked up his old violin.

THIRTY YEARS OF MAKING MAGIC OUT OF ORDINARINESS

Celebrating *Science Fiction World*'s Thirtieth Anniversary

TRANSLATED BY HENRY ZHANG

Written June 19, 2009, at Niangzi Pass
First published in *Science Fiction World: The 30th Anniversary Supplement* in September 2009

Science Literature (now known as *Science Fiction World*) has been an integral part of my life since its founding, from the craze for science fiction in the 1980s to the long chill in interest between then and now. But strangely enough, after promising the editor to write about these past three decades, I was unable to come up with much. Because I live so far away, my dealings with the magazine mostly consist in sending and receiving manuscripts; even today, I'm not acquainted with most of the staff, and I haven't learned anything about their personal lives or work lives. So even though most of my fiction this past decade has been published in *Science Fiction World*, the magazine remains as mysterious to me as it must be to ordinary readers.

I first learned of *Science Literature* in freshman year of college, in the eighties. I read about its inception in the news (I think it was *China Youth Daily*). I remember it was advertised as China's first "large-scale science fiction magazine." The story that stood out for me the most in the first few editions was "The Beta Mystery," an homage to *I, Robot*, though most readers then wouldn't have realized. It stood out not because of any particular sci-fi content, but because one of its characters, the director of a research institute, had worked as part of the underground resistance in Free China, during the Second Sino-Japanese War. I recently attended a local writers' association meeting where someone mentioned how incredibly rich and varied literature in the eighties was, even though it had just emerged from the prison of socialist realism. Stories about different types of people, and different socioeconomic classes, poured into publishing presses. But now, fiction has narrowed in scope and vision. This is the case with science fiction as well. In the eighties, despite how simple science fiction was from a literary perspective, the kinds of science it imagined were myriad. Just look at some of the stories published in *Science Literature*. They included exploiting the geothermal energy of the Himalayas, using infrasonic waves to exterminate pests, transferring human consciousness into a turtle's brain and displaying it holographically, using corn to harvest gold, and building environmentally friendly, smoke-ring-blowing chimneys, to name just some.

But another story that stood out to me had nothing to do with science fiction. I've forgotten its title. That day, I saw a roommate pick up my recently received copy of *Science Literature*, and express his appreciation for a particular story. When I took the magazine and looked, I wasn't even sure that what I was reading was fiction: it was the account of two people, an intellectual—a freedom fighter—and an old revolutionary. The intellectual marries the revolutionary, not by choice, but because her superiors force her. On the night of the marriage, a gunshot sounds from the bride and groom's bedroom. The story had nothing to do with science fiction, but did, in a sense, illuminate the predicament in which Chinese science fiction had landed itself. The story gave me a bad feeling about science fiction's future, and it wasn't long before my fears were confirmed, and Chinese science fiction entered a dark age.

I graduated and entered the workforce, joining the first batch of computer engineers to maintain the electric power system. Because life and work suddenly turned a lot more stressful, and Chinese science fiction was in such dire straits, I totally forgot about *Science Literature* for a while. A few years later, after work and life settled down a bit, I once again had leisure time. After losing an entire month's salary during a game of cards in the men's dormitory, I decided to pick up some old, less expensive hobbies, like science fiction; that was when I started writing *Supernova Era*. This was the nineties, and the seas of Chinese science fiction were deathly still, but I still picked up my ancient, dust-laden copy of *Science Literature*, and wrote a letter to the address on its cover, sure that the magazine had shut down, and that I was writing into the void. I never expected to receive such a quick reply, where I was told enthusiastically of the magazine's survival, and that it had changed names to *Exotic Tales*, and then to *Science Fiction World*.

I also received a complimentary copy of the magazine, and a stack of flyers that I was asked to read and then put up. These were poorly printed, monochrome ads. I'm ashamed to say that I didn't read them and lacked the nerve to share them, but thinking back, I wonder what people would have thought had such ads suddenly appeared overnight on the walls of our factory. But I've kept the ads to this day. That was obviously the most difficult period the magazine had gone through. The stories included were very short: one was about looking for the singularity at the beginning of the big bang, and another one was about a giant, living planet. They all showed a certain trend: Compared to the eighties, the writers' concerns had broadened, and the emphasis had changed from technological inventions to scientific theory. I sent back the thick, first draft of *Supernova Era* to the head of publishing, Yang Xiao, and even though she wasn't able to publish it (it was very hard to publish entire science fiction novels then), her enthusiasm and sincerity moved and encouraged me to keep writing.

When I sent the manuscript, I also asked for Zheng Wenguang's address; he'd been the person I most wanted to meet since middle school. But after receiving the information, I never got the chance to visit him. One night in 2002, when Beijing Normal University was hosting the Galaxy Awards, Yao Haijun and a few others decided to visit Mr. Zheng's house. At first, I was going to join them, but someone wanted to drag me to a dance party, and so I stayed behind, thinking there would be more chances to meet him. Alas, there weren't.

In 1999, I attended my first science fiction conference, and the one that left the deepest impression on me, not just because the senior editor of *Journal of Short Stories* gave a talk about literature, but also because it was the first time I spoke to people in person about science fiction, and saw them talk to each other about it. It was a strange, almost unreal moment. I went to more conferences, and what struck me the most was that the authors kept changing. Except for a few older writers, it seemed like each time, half the faces were new ones, whereas many people who'd shown up at one conference the previous year were nowhere to be seen. But after 2006, the ranks of fiction writers born in the eighties had basically stabilized. And the 2006 conference saw a major change: a crowd of people who looked entirely different than the science fiction writers appeared. They were fashionable and lively, in contrast to the melancholic, doom-obsessed sci-fi writers. These were the fantasy writers. It was an important transitional period for Chinese science fiction.

In truth, whether we're talking about science fiction across the globe or in China, it's far too early to get nostalgic. Even to an individual, thirty years is hardly a slog; the glories and obstacles of the past are just a speck compared to the vastness of the future. Nostalgia ages people, but science fiction is a literature of youth. Its spirit is the youthful yearning for new worlds, and new ways of living. Mainstream literature is like Chinese *baijiu,* tasting better as it ages; science fiction, on the other hand, is like tap beer—you've got to drink it quick. Read today, even sci-fi classics seem feeble, not revelatory. The nature of science fiction is to shine brightest in the present, then to be quickly forgotten. But science fiction shouldn't be afraid of obsolescence. As a literature of innovation, it uses a constant stream of inventions and shocks to hold back obsolescence, like an everlasting fire. Just as ash falls, the flame springs back to life, emitting dazzling light. To accomplish this, it must hold on to its youthfulness. Only tonight can we permit ourselves a moment of nostalgia. Tomorrow morning, we ought to try and return to a child's way of seeing things, and face that future of infinite possibilities that only children possess.

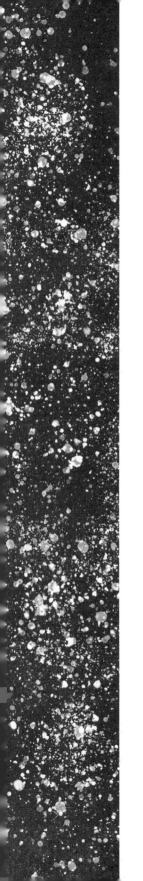

BUTTERFLY

TRANSLATED BY ELIZABETH HANLON

Written July 11, 1999, at Niangzi Pass
First published in *King of Science Fiction*, 2002, no. 1

The modern study of chaos began with the creeping realization in the 1960s that quite simple mathematical equations could model systems every bit as violent as a waterfall. Tiny differences in input could quickly become overwhelming differences in output—a phenomenon given the name "sensitivity dependence on initial conditions." In weather, for example, this translates into what is only half-jokingly known as the Butterfly Effect—the notion that a butterfly stirring the air today in Peking can transform storm systems next month in New York.

. . . Sensitive dependence on initial conditions was not an altogether new notion. It had a place in folklore:

> For want of a nail, the shoe was lost;
> For want of a shoe, the horse was lost;
> For want of a horse, the rider was lost;
> For want of a rider, the battle was lost;
> For want of a battle, the kingdom was lost!
> —James Gleick, *Chaos: Making a New Science*

MARCH 23, BELGRADE

Four-year-old Katya heard the first few explosions from her sickroom on the fifth floor of the Children's Hospital. She looked out the window, but the night sky appeared unchanged. Louder and more frightening than the dull blasts was the tumultuous sound of footsteps in the corridors, which seemed to shake the whole building.

Katya's mother Elena picked up her daughter and ran out of the room. They joined the crowd rushing through the ward in the direction of the basement. Her father Aleksandar and his Russian friend Reznik exited the room close behind them, but split off and ran upstairs, against the stream of people. Elena did not notice them. Over the past year, she had devoted her body and soul to Katya's care. She had donated one of her own kidneys in order to save her daughter from the ravages of uremia. Today was the day Katya was to be discharged from the hospital, and

Elena's joy at her daughter's new lease on life overrode any concerns about the outbreak of war.

But this was not the case for Aleksandar. When the explosions quieted, war would occupy his entire life. He stood next to Reznik on the roof of the building and surveyed the fires flickering to life in the distance. Overhead, the tracers of the antiaircraft guns punctuated the night with brilliant ellipses.

"There is a joke," said Aleksandar, "about a family who had a lovely, stubborn daughter. One day, the military erected barracks next to their home. The privates stationed there were a rakish bunch, and they often teased the girl, which caused her father to worry to no end. Before long, someone told him his daughter was pregnant! Upon hearing the news, he let out a long sigh of relief and said, 'Thank god, it finally happened.'"

"That is not a Russian joke," frowned Reznik.

"I didn't understand it at first either, but now I get it. When the thing you have feared for a long time happens, sometimes it comes as a relief."

"You are not God, Aleksandar."

"Or so I have been reminded by the bastards in the Department of Defense," Aleksandar replied dryly.

"You are saying you went to the government? They did not believe you could find the atmospheric sensitivity points?"

"Can you believe it?"

"Not at first, but I came around once I saw how your mathematical model operated."

"Nobody there will look closely at my model, but they mostly don't believe me anyway."

"But you are not opposed to the party."

"I'm not anything! I'm not interested in politics. Maybe it's because I mouthed off during the civil war years."

By now, the sound of explosions had ceased, but the fires in the distance had grown brighter, suffusing the two tallest buildings in the city with a dull red glow. The towers stood on opposite banks of the Sava River. In New Belgrade, the white façade of the headquarters of the Socialist Party of Serbia stood out against the flames. Across the river loomed the specter of the Belgrade Palace, its black exterior indistinct, like a strange reflection of the first building.

"Theoretically speaking, your model might work, but there is something you may have overlooked," Reznik mused. "To calculate one sensitivity point for the weather of the whole country and its activation mechanism, even with all of Yugoslavia's fastest computers, would take a month or more to complete."

"That is exactly the reason I came to find you. I want to use that computer of yours in Dubna."

"What makes you so certain I will agree?"

"I'm not certain. But your grandfather was a military adviser to Tito, and he was wounded at the Battle of Sutjeska."

"Fine. But how will I obtain the initial atmospheric data for the entire globe?"

"It's public. You can download it from the World Meteorological Network. The feed aggregates real-time data from every weather satellite around the world, as well as every participating observation point on land and sea. It's a huge volume of data, though, so a phone line won't cut it. You'll need a dedicated cable with a transmission rate of at least a million bits per second."

"This I have."

Aleksandar handed Reznik a small briefcase with a combination lock. "Everything God himself might possibly need is inside, but the CD is the most important thing. I burned a copy of my atmospheric modeling software, about six hundred megabytes, or almost the entire capacity of the disc. It's the uncompiled C language source code, so your monster machine ought to be able to run it," he explained. "There's also a satellite phone connected to a modified GPS receiver. With this, you can see my precise location anywhere on Earth."

Reznik took the case and said, "I leave tonight for Romania to catch a flight to Moscow. If everything goes smoothly, I will call you on the satellite phone by this time tomorrow to share the details of your miracle sensitivity point. But I doubt its effect can be amplified as planned. Commanding the elements is really best left to God."

After Reznik departed, Aleksandar left the hospital and returned home with his wife and daughter. When they reached the confluence of the

Sava and Danube Rivers, he stopped the car, and the three of them got out to quietly observe the dark surface of the water.

After a long silence, Aleksandar spoke: "I said once that when war broke out, I would have to leave home."

"Are you scared of the bombs, Papa? Take me with you, I'm scared, too. They are really loud!" said Katya.

"No, sweetie, I am going to find a way to stop the bombs from falling on our land. Papa may have to go somewhere far away, so he can't bring Katya. Actually, Papa doesn't even know where he will go."

"How will you stop the bombs from falling? Can you find a strong army to protect us?"

"There's no need for an army, Katya. Papa just needs to do one little thing at the right time and right place on Earth, like pouring a bucket of hot water or smoking a cigar, and all of Yugoslavia will be covered by clouds and fog. Then the bombs and the people who drop them won't be able to find their targets!"

"Why are you telling her this?" Elena cut in.

"It doesn't matter. No one will believe her, including you."

"A year ago, you went to the Australian coast and turned on an industrial fan, under the delusion that this would bring rain to dusty Ethiopia . . ."

"I didn't succeed that time, but it wasn't because of errors in my theory or my mathematical model. I didn't have a computer that was fast enough, so in the time it took to calculate the sensitivity point, atmospheric variation had already desensitized it!"

"Aleksandar, you are always living in a dream! But I will not stand in your way. I would not have married you if those dreams had not moved me once . . ." Elena recalled the past in mute sorrow. She had been born into a Muslim household in Bosnia. Five years ago, when she fled the besieged city of Sarajevo and wed her Serbian college classmate, her obstinate father and brother had nearly turned their Kalashnikovs on her.

After he drove Elena and Katya home, Aleksandar turned his car toward Romania. It was not an easy drive. The road was snarled with checkpoints and wartime traffic, and he did not cross the border until noon the next day. It was smooth sailing thereafter, and he arrived at Bucharest Otopeni International Airport before nightfall.

MARCH 25, DUBNA

One hundred miles to the north of Moscow, there was a small town untainted by the decadence and decline of the capital. The spruce little town reposed amid meadows and dappled shade. Here, the passage of time had stopped, as evidenced by scattered busts of Lenin. At the entrance to the town, the mouth of the tunnel that ran beneath the Volga River was still adorned with a Soviet-era slogan in big letters: LABOR IS GLORIOUS. Sixty thousand people lived here, and almost all of them were scientists. The town was called Dubna, and it was home to the former Soviet Union's research center for high technology and nuclear weapons.

In the center of town stood a newly constructed building, whose elegant, even avant-garde appearance offered a striking contrast to the Soviet-style architecture around it. There was a fully enclosed computer lab on the second floor of the building, which was unexpectedly equipped with an American-made Cray supercomputer. Although it was an older model, at the time it belonged to the list of equipment strictly prohibited from export to the Eastern Bloc under the now-defunct COMECON. Four years prior, with Russia's cooperation, the United States, the United Kingdom, Germany, and France jointly established a high-technology research center. It was the Western countries' hope that generous compensation and a good research environment might tempt Russian scientists away from non-Western countries, particularly those nuclear physicists who could otherwise earn only a measly hundred US dollars per month. At the same time, Russia and the West would share the fruits of the center's research. The building in Dubna was merely a branch facility of the larger center. Due to Russia's lagging supercomputing infrastructure, researchers faced considerable operational difficulties. To remedy the situation, the Americans installed the Cray supercomputer. The huge machine was controlled by US engineers, who were also responsible for vetting any software that ran on it.

If the computer could feel, it would certainly have felt lonely. Since it had taken up residence here three years ago, the vast majority of its time was spent idling, or periodically running self-diagnostic tests. There were a handful of graduate students from the Moscow State University College of Electronics who occasionally fed it computation programs via the terminal on the first floor, but if it ever slept, it might have handled those programs in its sleep just as easily.

Late in the evening of March 25, the Cray supercomputer received a program written in C language from the network terminal, followed by a compilation command. It was an enormous piece of software—the largest it had ever seen, in fact—but the computer remained unenthused. It had seen programs containing more than ten million lines of code before, only to discover at runtime that most of the code represented mechanized loops and pixel conversions, designed to generate uninspired 3-D animation models. It launched the compiler and began absently translating line after line of C code into the ones and zeros of its native tongue, funneling the unimaginably long string of numbers into external storage. Just as it finished compiling the code, it received a command to execute. The computer immediately sucked the mountain of ones and zeros it had spat out only moments before back into its internal memory. Plucking a fine thread from the tangled skein of code, it began to run the program.

There was a sharp, involuntary intake of breath and a shudder from the Cray supercomputer. In an instant, the program had spawned over a million high-order matrices, three million ordinary differential equations, and eight million partial differential equations. The little mathematical monsters stretched their greedy maws wide and waited for the initial data. Soon, a torrent of data began to surge through a separate 10 Mbps transmission channel. The computer could just barely distinguish the elements that composed the flood—set after set of pressure, temperature, and humidity parameters. The initial data, like incandescent lava, flowed into the sea of matrices and equations and set everything to a seething boil. Each of the supercomputer's thousand-plus CPUs reached maximum capacity. A typhoon of logic howled across the vast electronic world of its memory, whipping up turbid, monstrous waves of data.

The storm lasted for forty minutes, which, to the computer, seemed like centuries. At last, it let out a breath. Stretching its power to the limit, it narrowly conquered the raging world within. The typhoon slackened, and the breakers gradually subsided. Soon, the typhoon dispersed completely, and the sea began to solidify and shrink rapidly. It finally condensed into a tiny kernel of data, which twinkled continuously in the boundless void of the computer's internal memory. Then, the seed split open, displaying a few lines of data on the screen of the first-floor terminal.

From where he sat in front of the screen, Reznik picked up the satellite phone.

"The first sensitivity point has appeared. It is drifting in the area bounded by latitudes twenty-two degrees and twenty-five degrees north and longitudes thirteen degrees and fifteen degrees west. Activation mechanism: Sharply cool the sensitivity point. Where is it? Let me see . . . Oh! You must go to Africa, Aleksandar!"

MARCH 27, MAURITANIA

As the helicopter skimmed low over the sunbaked desert, Aleksandar thought he might suffocate in the sweltering heat. The pilot, however, seemed completely unfazed. He kept up a steady stream of chatter the entire way. This peculiar white man had piqued his curiosity. After stepping off his flight at Nouakchott International Airport, the man had immediately engaged the service of his light helicopter. Then, he had purchased a freezer from a restaurant next to the terminal, in which he placed a large block of ice. Finally, he had loaded both the freezer and a large sledgehammer into the helicopter. The man could not identify his destination, and had simply directed him to fly the helicopter into the desert in the direction in which he pointed. He kept a large, strange-looking phone pressed to his ear the entire flight. The phone was connected to what looked like a game console. The pilot had seen a similar device when he had worked for a copper-prospecting team, and he knew it was a GPS receiver.

"Hey, friend, you came from Cairo?!" the pilot shouted over the pulsing roar of the engine in stilted French.

"I came from the Balkans, and changed planes in Cairo," answered Aleksandar, only half listening.

"*Pardon?* The Balkans! There's a war on, yes?"

"Seems like it."

Six thousand kilometers away, Reznik's voice in Aleksandar's earpiece informed him that his position was clear. The sensitivity point had stabilized, and was currently drifting very slowly at a distance of five kilometers.

"The Americans have dropped many bombs there, even Tomahawks, no?" The pilot imitated the sound of a missile whizzing overhead, followed by a cartoonish explosion. "Hey, friend, do you know how much one Tomahawk costs?"

"One and a half million US dollars, I think."

Aleksandar, pay attention. Just thirty-five hundred meters to go.

"Wow! White people are always so extravagant. That much money here could build a plantation, or a reservoir. It could feed a lot of people, no?"

Three thousand meters, Aleksandar!

The pilot continued. "Why is America fighting? You don't know?! Oh, I heard Milošević killed four thousand people in someplace called Kosovo . . ."

Two thousand meters, Aleksandar. It's drifting again, to the left!

"Turn left!" barked Aleksandar.

". . . what? Left? Okay, is this all right?"

Aleksandar repeated the question to Reznik. *Ah, too far to the left.*

"Too far, bring it back a little bit!"

"You should give me a clear direction," the pilot grumbled. "Are we okay now?"

"Okay, Reznik?" Aleksandar muttered into the satellite phone. *Dead ahead, Aleksandar. Fifteen hundred meters to go.* "Perfect, hold it steady. Thank you, friend."

"Do not mention it. You are paying me a very fair price! Oh, as I was saying, he killed four thousand people. But, do you remember, two years ago there was killing in Africa, too . . ."

One thousand meters!

". . . in Rwanda . . ."

Five hundred meters!

". . . killed five hundred thousand people . . ."

One hundred meters!

". . . did anyone care? . . ."

Aleksandar, you are on top of the sensitivity point!

"Land the helicopter!" Aleksandar interrupted.

". . . you have probably already forgotten it . . . what, land it? Here? Got it! I hope the sand will not trap the landing skids . . . Okay, you have arrived. Wait a moment before you get out, or you will be blinded!"

With the pilot's assistance, Aleksandar lifted the freezer down from the cabin, and then pulled out the ice block that had already started to melt and placed it on the sand. All around them, the desert shimmered in the blistering heat.

"Take care not to burn yourself," chuckled the pilot, as Aleksandar raised the sledgehammer over the ice.

For my suffering homeland, I flap the wings of a butterfly . . .

He silently mouthed the phrase in Serbian, his eyes half closed. Then, he brought the hammer crashing down onto the ice, shattering the block into glittering shards, which melted on contact with the sand, like a fleeting reverie. A cool, invigorating draft rose and dispersed, quickly engulfed by the hot desert air.

"What on earth are you doing, friend?" The pilot eyed him with a bemused look on his face.

"A ritual of sorts. A totemic rite, like your fire dances," laughed Aleksandar, wiping sweat from his brow.

"The ritual, and that mysterious spell—you are praying to your god for something?"

"Rain and fog, rain and fog to cover my distant homeland."

MARCH 29, BELGRADE

It was Katya's best night of sleep yet. Her body had rejected her new kidney, and she had grown feverish. After her mother asked a neighbor who worked as a nurse to administer an immunosuppressant injection brought back from the hospital, she felt a little better. More importantly, that evening, the thunder of explosions diminished to a few scattered rumbles, and the residents of their apartment building did not bolt to the basement at midnight to wait for dawn. The next day, Katya discovered the reason why.

That morning, Katya got up late. It was already past eight, but it was still very dark outside. She went out onto the balcony and saw that the sky was overcast with dark, heavy clouds. Streamers of mist twined through the trees.

"My God . . ." Elena uttered a low cry at the sight.

"Mama, did Papa do this?"

"Probably not. But if it stays cloudy for a few weeks, then maybe he really did it."

"Where is Papa now?"

"I don't know. He is a butterfly, winging his way around the world."

"There are no butterflies that ugly!" Katya pronounced. "Anyway, I don't like cloudy days."

MARCH 29, ALLIED AIR FORCES COMBAT DIRECTIVE NO. 1362

Sent from: AIRCOM Operations Center.

Full text distributed to: AFSOUTH, SETAF, and Commanding General, US 6th Fleet.

Intelligence Report M441 from sources EAM and NM* proved erroneous (see Field Conditions Database "ASD119," meteorological section), and was corrected in Intelligence Report M483.

Combat Directives No. 1351, No. 1353, and No. 1357 are hereby amended as follows.

The following section was distributed to all Forward Operating Bases in: Italy (Comiso, Aviano, Caserma Ederle, La Maddalena, Sigonella, Brisindi) and Greece (Souda Bay, Iraklion, Athens, Nea Makri).

It was also forwarded to: Mediterranean Carrier Strike Group.

Cancel all B3† strikes issued under Combat Directives No. 1351 and No. 1357 against target groups GH56, IIT773, NT4412, BBH091145, LO88, 1123RRT, and 691HJ (indexed under "TAG471" in Target Database).

Continue B3 strikes issued under Combat Directive No. 1353 against target groups PA851 and SSF67 (see index above).

....

* EAM and NM refer respectively to the US Air Force Europe Weather Agency and the US National Weather Service.

† Refers to laser-guided missiles and television-guided missiles.

A2‡ *strikes issued under Combat Directives No. 1351, No. 1353, and No. 1357 remain in effect.*

The following section was distributed to: Aviano Air Base.

Increase low-altitude observation flights to evaluate the AF3 effects of the remaining B3 strikes.

TOP SECRET

Number of Copies: 0

MARCH 29, DUBNA

"Aleksandar, Aleksandar! Listen, the second sensitivity point has formed, between latitudes twenty-nine degrees and thirty degrees north and longitudes one hundred and thirty-three degrees and one hundred and thirty-four degrees west. It is moving fast, but it is stabilizing. Activation mechanism: Violently disturb the water. Oh, it is out at sea, you know."

MARCH 31, OFF THE WEST COAST OF THE RYUKYU ISLANDS

The surface of the sea was calm and smooth like blue satin. The little fishing vessel was traveling at full speed, cutting a long, foaming wake behind it.

On the aft deck, an Okinawan fisherman, skin dark from exposure, was busy wrapping a bundle of TNT in waterproof paper. His equally leathery partner had set about connecting the electric blasting cap that was strapped to the explosive to an igniter with a long fuse wire. Aleksandar stood to the side and looked on. The two men chatted while they worked. Out of respect for Aleksandar, they spoke in accented but fluent English. Like the rest of the world, their discussion revolved around war.

"I think it's good news for us," said one of the men. "Sets a precedent. If a problem with North Korea or Taiwan arises in the future, our Saberhawks and the Americans' aircraft carrier can cruise up, guns blazing. Magnificent!"

....

‡ Refers to Tomahawk cruise missiles.

"Fucking Americans, I can't stand them! They can get the hell out of Okinawa, and they can take their noisy planes, too!"

"Use your head, you idiot. If there was no military base, who would buy our fish? More importantly, you're Japanese. You should consider what's best for Japan."

"How do I put this? Iwata-kun, you and I are different. Your family came over from Kyushu ten years ago, but as for me, my family has lived in Okinawa for generations. It was once an independent kingdom, which makes you and the Americans outsiders."

"Hirose-kun, just listen to yourself. Governor Ota is full of shit, and you're not the first person he has led astray . . . Oh, mister, it's ready."

Aleksandar carried the neatly wrapped explosive to the stern. Pressing the satellite phone to his ear, he waited.

"Mister, if you want to catch fish with that thing, listen to me and pick a different direction!"

"I don't want to blast any fish, just the water," replied Aleksandar.

"It's your money, so we'll do it your way, of course. There are more and more weirdos like you visiting Okinawa these days."

Aleksandar, Aleksandar! You are on top of the sensitivity point! Create a disturbance!

Aleksandar cast the explosive into the sea.

"Careful! Don't let the wire foul the propeller!" yelled one of the fishermen, as the fuse wire uncoiled and snaked rapidly over the stern. Aleksandar placed a finger on the trigger button.

For my suffering homeland, I flap the wings of a butterfly . . .

There was a dull, shuddering roar from beneath the surface, and a huge column of water erupted thirty meters from the stern, white spray glittering in the sunlight. The great mass of water fell back into the sea, and the surface boiled and frothed for a time, but soon everything was quiet again.

"I told you you wouldn't catch anything," muttered one of the Okinawans, gazing at the smooth patch of sea.

APRIL 1, BELGRADE

"Mama, it's been cloudy for three days now! It must be Papa!" exclaimed Katya from where she stood by the window.

The pale sky of the last two days had grown dark and steely, and the clouds pressed low against the city. The white tower and the black palace, shrouded in fog, stood sentry over the Sava River in the drizzling rain.

Elena shook her head. "I am convinced it is an act of God."

APRIL 1, AIRSPACE OVER YUGOSLAVIA, F-117 ATTACK SQUADRON

Forward Air Controller: "Black Beauty, Black Beauty, you are flying over your target."

F-117: "Cyclops, Cyclops, target visibility is zero. I am flying above the clouds at forty-five hundred meters."

Forward Air Controller: "I am flying below the clouds at eighteen hundred meters. I have just tested the laser target designator. The target cannot be identified with sufficient accuracy to initiate an airstrike. The fog is too thick."

F-117: "Cyclops, test television guidance."

Forward Air Controller: "Testing television guidance . . . Black Beauty, the target can be identified with sufficient accuracy. You will have to descend through the cloud layer to attack. Cloud base over the target is at two thousand meters."

F-117: "I am ready to strike. Cyclops, please record blast damage."

Forward Air Controller: "Black Beauty, Black Beauty, do not descend! Artillery fire is heavy below the clouds, and I am detecting Tamala radiation[§] on the ground!"

F-117: "Cyclops, I am going in low. We cannot return empty-handed again!"

....

§ Tamala radar was a system produced by the Czechs that utilized unique "passive detection" methods. It was said to be capable of detecting F-117 and B-2 stealth fighter jets, and also, that it was deeply feared by the Allied Air Forces.

Forward Air Controller: "Black Beauty, pull up! Remember the rules of engagement! Major Grant, do you want to be court-martialed?!"

Grant pulled the control stick back toward his chest, and then tilted it to the right. The angular black body of the F-117 rose lazily upward and then made a sudden, sharp turn, streaking across the vast expanse of clouds in the direction of Italy. Inside his helmet, Grant sighed.

Damn, before I took off from Aviano, I signed my name on those two MK-12 laser-guided bombs below me.

APRIL 1, ALLIED AIR FORCES COMBAT DIRECTIVE NO. 1694
From: AIRCOM Operations Center.

Full text distributed to: AFSOUTH, SETAF, and CG, US 6th Fleet.

Intelligence Reports M769 and M770 from sources EAM and NM proved erroneous for a second time (see Field Conditions Database "ASD119," meteorological section). The intelligence reliability rating of the aforementioned sources has been reduced from T1 to T3.

Combat Directives No. 1681 through No. 1690 are hereby amended according to Post-Strike Aerial Damage Assessment ND224 and ground intelligence from S24.

The following section was distributed to all Forward Operating Bases in Italy (Comiso, Aviano, Caserma Ederle, La Maddalena, Sigonella, Brisindi) and Greece (Souda Bay, Iraklion, Athens, Nea Makri).

It was also forwarded to: Mediterranean Carrier Strike Group.

Cancel all B3 strikes issued under Combat Directive No. 1681 and all subsequent Directives against target groups TA67 through TA71, 110LK, TU81, GH1632, SPT4418, MH703, and BR45 through BR67 (indexed under "TAG471" in Target Database).

TOP SECRET

Number of Copies: 0

APRIL 2, DUBNA
"Aleksandar, the third sensitivity point! Region: Bounded by latitudes seventy-six degrees and seventy-seven degrees south and longitudes

ninety-two degrees and ninety-three degrees east. Activation mechanism: Sharply raise the temperature of the sensitivity point.

"You must go to Antarctica, friend. First go to Puerto Natales, Patagonia, but do not charter a vessel. There is not enough time! I have a friend there who was on the team that conducted the last survey of the Antarctic ozone hole. He is very resourceful. He has a private plane, and can fly you directly to the sensitivity point in Marie Byrd Land. He might still have a foothold there. It may take some time for you to catch up to this sensitivity point, and when you do, the effect of the second point will likely have faded. We must let the skies over your country clear up for two or three days. But do not worry—this sensitivity point is very stable. It will not drift too far, and it can last for a long time, which may be related to Antarctica's constant freezing temperatures. More importantly, it can be activated multiple times! This way, you can stay there—naturally, it will not be very comfortable—and in half a month clouds and fog will cover the Balkans!

"Well done, Aleksandar, unbelievably well done!"

APRIL 4, BELGRADE

"It's sunny, Mama!" squealed Katya, looking at the blue sky from the balcony.

Elena released a small sigh. "Aleksandar, you're not really the Messiah."

There was a huge roar followed by the sound of rattling glass. Another roar, and dust showered down from the ceiling.

"Katya, we need to get to the basement!"

"No," whined the little girl, "I like sunny days!"

APRIL 6, MARIE BYRD LAND, ANTARCTICA

"What a pure and quiet world! I could stay here forever," exclaimed Aleksandar.

From two thousand meters above, the endless ice sheet was tinged with a faint, bewitching blue by the hazy sun on the horizon.

The pilot, a strapping Argentinian man named Alfonso, glanced at Aleksandar and said, "This purity will be gone soon. Tourism in

Antarctica is developing rapidly. At first, it was limited to the Shetland Islands, but now it is expanding inland. Sea cruises and scenic flights are arriving in droves. My tour company is thriving, and I will never have to fish or ranch like my father's generation."

"But it's not just tourism—isn't your government planning to allow immigration to the mainland?"

"Why not? After all, Argentina is the closest country to Antarctica! The world is going to leave this land battered and bleeding sooner or later, just like what's happening in the Balkans."

Just then, Reznik's voice came over the satellite phone connection: *Aleksandar, we have a small problem. The Americans have closed off access to the Cray computer lab!*

"Do you think we've been detected?"

Not at all. I told them we were running a piece of global atmospheric modeling software, which is true. Relations with the West are strained right now, and the research center was bound to feel the effects. You stay put—I will straighten things out soon.

As the plane coasted to a halt on the snowy plain, Aleksandar saw a small cabin up ahead. The cabin was constructed from thermal insulation boards, and was raised on four upright posts to prevent the accumulation of snowdrifts.

"This was left here by a British survey team, and I fixed the place up a little," said Alfonso, pointing to the outpost. "There's enough food and fuel inside to last us a month."

APRIL 7, BELGRADE

Katya's body had rejected the transplant again. The fever had returned, and the little girl mumbled fitfully in her sleep. The injections Elena had brought home on the day of Katya's discharge had been used up, and she would have to return to the hospital to replenish their supply. The hospital was all the way on the other side of the city.

It was another sunny day.

"Mama, tell me a story before you go." Katya propped herself up in bed and took her mother's arm.

"Sweetie, Mama has already told you all the fairy tales she knows.

Mama will tell you one last story, but Katya is a big girl now, and after this there will be no more.

"In the not-so-distant past, only three years before Katya was born, we lived in a much bigger country than we do now. Our country stretched almost all the way down the eastern shore of the Adriatic Sea. In this country, Serbians, Croatians, Slovenians, Macedonians, Montenegrins, and Bosnians were one big family. They lived together in peace and harmony, and treated each other like brothers and sisters . . ."

"Even the Albanians in Kosovo?"

"Yes, even the Albanians. A powerful man called Tito led our country. We were strong and proud, and our culture was rich and colorful. The whole world respected us . . ."

Elena stared absently at the patch of blue sky outside the window, tears glistening in the corners of her eyes.

"Then what happened?" asked Katya.

Elena stood. "Child, stay at home and rest while I am gone. If the bombs come, listen to Uncle Letnić next door. Don't forget to put on more clothes before you go to the basement, or the cold and damp will aggravate your illness." She picked up her bag and walked out the door.

"What happened to the country?" Katya called after her mother's retreating figure.

There was no gas in the family car, so Elena had to take a taxi. She had to wait much longer than usual, but she still managed to hail a passing cab. It was a relatively smooth ride. There were few other cars and people on the streets, and plumes of smoke were visible in the distance. When she arrived at the Children's Hospital, she discovered that the shelling had left the hospital without power. Nurses stood clustered in the premature infant station, delivering oxygen to the sealed incubators by hand. Medicine was in short supply, but she was able to retrieve the immunosuppressants Katya needed.

As soon as she had the drugs in hand, Elena rushed back. This time, she waited even longer for a taxi, and in the end, she had to catch a ride on a mostly empty bus. When she spotted the Danube River from the window, Elena let out a sigh of relief. She was already halfway home. The sky was vast and cloudless, and the city sat beneath it like a target painted on the surface of Earth.

"You are not the Messiah, Aleksandar," Elena muttered inwardly.

The bus drove onto a bridge that spanned the Danube. In the absence of other traffic, it soon reached the center. A cool river breeze was blowing through the bus window, and Elena could not smell the gun smoke. Except for the distant trickles of smoke, the city seemed tranquil in the bright sunshine, perhaps even more so than before.

It was then that Elena saw it.

She saw it low above the ground in the distance. At first, it appeared as a black speck that flashed against the background of the blue sky; as it grew closer, she could make out its elongated form. It cruised through the air at a steady pace. Elena had not imagined that it would fly so slowly, as if it were searching for something. It dipped low over the river, tracing a graceful arc through the air. Elena had to peer downward to see it skimming along the river's surface. It was close enough that Elena could clearly see its smooth, innocuous exterior. It did not resemble the ferocious shark described by the newspapers; it was closer to a guileless, innocent dolphin that had leapt clear of the Danube's waters.

The Tomahawk missile struck the bridge and brought it crashing down into the Danube. Days later, when the overturned bus was removed from the river, rescue workers recovered the charred corpses of several passengers. Among them was the body of a woman, her arms still clutched tightly around a handbag that contained two boxes of injections. Even in death, she had protected the handbag well: half of the syringes had not shattered, and the prescription name was still visible on the labels of the boxes. The firefighter in charge of the salvage efforts remarked that it was an uncommon drug.

APRIL 7, MARIE BYRD LAND, ANTARCTICA

"I'll teach you how to dance the tango," said Alfonso, and so he and Aleksandar sprang to their feet and whirled across the snow. Here, it was as if Aleksandar had stumbled onto another planet. In the perpetual twilight of the snowfield, he forgot the passage of time, even forgot the war.

"You dance quite well, but that is not a real Argentinian tango."

"I can never get the head snaps right."

"That's because you don't understand the meaning of the movements. When Argentinian cowboys first began to dance the tango, they did not move their heads. Later, the cowboys who crowded around to watch the dance grew jealous of the cowboys with pretty girls on their arms, so they began to pelt them with stones. So from then on, you had no choice but to stay vigilant and swivel your head in all directions."

Aleksandar's laughter trailed off into a deep sigh. "Yes, that's the way of the outside world."

APRIL 10, DUBNA

"Aleksandar, things have gone south. The Western countries have halted all cooperation projects at the research center, and the Americans plan to dismantle and remove the Cray supercomputer . . . I am trying to find a way to access another computer. There is a nuclear detonation simulation center in Dubna. It is a military facility, and they have a supercomputer there. A Russian-made machine might run more slowly, but it should be adequate to complete these calculations. But I need to run this idea by my superiors, and it might need to go even higher. Hold on for two more days! Though we cannot track it, I believe the sensitivity point is still in Antarctica!"

APRIL 13, BELGRADE

In the dim basement, which trembled with the force of the dull explosions above, Katya was fighting for every last breath.

The neighbors had exhausted every possibility. Two days prior, Uncle Letnić had sent his own son out to get the drugs, but the shelves of every hospital in the city were bare. The injections could only be imported from Western Europe—a virtual impossibility now.

There had been no news of Katya's mother.

In her stupor, Katya cried out for her mother over and over again, but it was her father who appeared in the remnants of her consciousness. He transformed into an immense butterfly, with wings as broad as football fields. As he ceaselessly flapped his enormous wings high overhead, the clouds and fog dissipated, and the sun shone brightly over Belgrade and the Danube . . .

"I like sunny days . . ." Katya mumbled.

APRIL 17, DUBNA

"Aleksandar, we have failed. I could not obtain access to the super-computer. Yes, I appealed the matter to the highest level through my channels at the Academy of Sciences, but . . . No, no, no. They did not say they disbelieved it, nor did they say they believed it. It is not import-ant either way. I have been dismissed from my post. They drove off an academician like a stray dog, and you ask why? Because I played a part in all this . . . Yes, they permitted a volunteer force to enter Yugoslavia, but what I did was different . . . I do not know, either. They are politi-cians, and we will never be able to understand the inner workings of their minds, just like they will never understand us . . . Don't be naïve. Believe me, it is absolutely impossible. There are only a few computers in the entire world that can complete such complicated calculations in a short time . . .

"Go home? No, do not go back. Katya . . . how can I tell you this, my friend? Katya passed three days ago. The rejection reaction took her in the end. Elena went to fetch medicine from the hospital eight days ago and never came back. No one has heard from her since . . . I do not know. It was not easy to get through to your home telephone. I heard this from your neighbors. Aleksandar, my friend, come to Moscow! Come to my home. We still have your software, at least, and it can change the world!

"Hello? Hello? Aleksandar!

". . . . . ."

APRIL 14, MARIE BYRD LAND, ANTARCTICA

"Alfonso, you go back to Argentina. I want to be here alone." Standing in front of the cabin on the snowfield, Aleksandar wore a sorrowful smile. "Thank you for everything you have done. Truly, thank you."

"You aren't from Greece, as Reznik claimed." Alfonso stared at Aleksandar. "You are from Yugoslavia. I don't know what you came here to do, but I am certain it is connected to the war."

"I suppose it was, but it doesn't matter anymore."

"I read it on your face when you were listening to the news on the radio. I saw that expression many times a decade ago on the Islas Malvi-nas. Back then I was a soldier, and I fought heroically. Yes, I was very brave. All of Argentina was very brave. We did not lack for courage and zeal, just a few Exocets . . . I still remember the day we surrendered. It was cloudy on the island that day—cloudy and wet and cold. But it was not so bad, the British let us keep our guns." Alfonso paused. "Very well, friend, I will return in a few days. Do not stray too far from the cabin. There have been many storms lately."

Aleksandar watched Alfonso's plane vanish into the white Antarctic sky, and then turned and went into the cabin. A moment later, he emerged with a bucket.

He never entered the cabin again.

Bucket in hand, Aleksandar walked aimlessly across the vast plain of snow. He did not know how much time had passed before he came to a halt.

. . . *Activation mechanism: Sharply raise the temperature of the sensitivity point.*

He opened the bucket, and fumbled for a lighter with frozen fingers.

For my suffering homeland, I flap the wings of a butterfly . . .

He lit the gasoline in the bucket, and then sat down in the snow and gazed at the rising flames. It was an ordinary fire. It lacked the intensity to activate the sensitivity point, and it would not bring clouds and fog to his homeland.

> *For want of a nail, the shoe was lost;*
> *For want of a shoe, the horse was lost;*
> *For want of a horse, the rider was lost;*
> *For want of a rider, the battle was lost;*
> *For want of a battle, the kingdom was lost!*

JULY 10, AFSOUTH HEADQUARTERS, ITALY

When it was all over, the weekend dance was reinstated, and the men could finally strip off the fatigues they had worn for three long months and don crisp dress uniforms. Between the grand marble columns of the Renaissance hall, the gold stars of the general officers and the silver stars of the field officers glimmered under the soft light of an enormous crystal chandelier. The ladies of Italian high society, who were not only glamorous but well-read and quick to engage in witty repartee, dotted the hall like blossoms. Together with the scintillating flow of wine, their presence made for an intoxicating night. Everyone congratulated themselves for having participated in such a glorious and romantic expedition.

When General Wesley Clark appeared in the company of his staff, the hall erupted into applause. The applause conferred upon him was not just in recognition of his meritorious service during the war. General Clark cut a tall, lean figure, and had the refined bearing of a scholar. He stood in marked contrast with the last war's General Schwarzkopf.

After two waltzes, the partygoers began to square dance. It was a popular dance within the Pentagon, but most of the ladies were unfamiliar with the steps, so the younger officers very enthusiastically began to teach them. General Clark decided to step out for a stroll. He left through a side entrance and came to a small lake in a vineyard. Another figure slipped out of the hall behind the general and followed him at a discreet distance. The general wound his way along the path through the secluded garden to the water's edge, seemingly entranced by the beautiful evening landscape.

But without warning, he spoke: "Hello, Colonel White."

The general's keen sixth sense caught White off guard, and he hastily stepped forward and saluted. "You still recognize me, General, sir?"

General Clark did not turn to face him. "I was very impressed by your work these past three months, Colonel. You and everyone else in the situation room have my thanks."

"General, please forgive me for interrupting, but there is a matter I wish to discuss with you. It's . . . rather personal. If I don't raise it now, I'm afraid I may not get another chance."

"By all means, tell me."

"Over the first few days of the campaign, some of the meteorological intelligence from the target zone was . . . a bit unreliable."

"Not unreliable, Colonel, just plain wrong," corrected the general. "We were left twiddling our thumbs through four days of rain and fog. If the forecast had been accurate, we would have delayed the first strike."

The sun had set some time ago, and mountains in the distance cut black silhouettes against the lingering twilight. The lake was mirror-calm, and a gondolier's song drifted across the water . . . It was a poor occasion for this sort of discussion, but the colonel knew this was his only opportunity, so he kept on talking.

"But some people will not let the matter drop. The Senate Armed Services Committee wants to know how the Air Force Weather Agency spent its two-billion-dollar budget over the last three years. They have formed an investigative subcommittee, and they want to hold hearings. It looks like they want to make a big show of it."

"I don't want it to blow out of proportion, but someone needs to be held responsible, Colonel."

White was sweating profusely. "That's not fair, sir. Everyone knows forecasting is a tremendously random business. The atmosphere is a complex chaotic system, and it's almost impossible to predict its behavior . . ."

"Colonel, if I remember correctly, you are responsible for target discrimination, which bears no relation to meteorology."

"That's right, sir, but . . . Colonel Katherine Davey of the USAF-E Weather Agency was responsible for meteorological intelligence in the Balkan target zone . . ." White hesitated. "Uh, you've seen her, she often comes to the Operations Center."

"Ah, yes, I remember, the doctor from Massachusetts." Clark suddenly whirled around. "Very tall, olive skin, slender legs—a beauty."

"Yes, sir, I . . ." White began, but the general interrupted his stammering.

"Colonel, I recall you said this was a personal matter."

White did not answer.

General Clark wore a stern expression. "Colonel, not only do I remember your name, but I also remember that you are married. I also know that your wife is not Colonel Davey."

"Yes, General, but . . . this is not America."

General Clark nearly burst out laughing, but he held back. He could not bear to destroy the quiet beauty of the place.

Afterword: The events described in this story are beyond the realm of possibility, not because of the limitations of human ability, but because

of fundamental impossibilities in the fields of physics and mathematics. One of the charms of science fiction, however, is that it can change the laws of nature and then show how the universe would operate according to those revisions.

ONE AND ONE HUNDRED THOUSAND THOUSAND EARTHS

TRANSLATED BY JESSE FIELD

Written October 29, 2011, at Niangzi Pass
First published in *Modern Weekly*, 2012, New Year Special

Compared to those of other animals, human infants are certainly weak. Infant horses can stand and walk on their own just ten minutes after birth, but human infants stay in their cradles a very long time, and during this period, if there is no outside party to take good care of them, they won't survive. On their own strengths, humans would never make it out of the cradle. The factors producing this phenomenon are the requirements of evolution, with the bulk of the human brain so big, it would be difficult to grow it after sexual maturity, so it must be grown before. All of which is to say: All human infants are born premature.

If we see human civilization as an infant, then it, too, was born premature. The pace of civilization's development is much faster than that of natural evolution, and humanity has in fact entered modern civilization with the brain and body of primitive humans. This leads us to a scary question: If no external world looks after it, will the human civilization be forever unable to step out of its cradle?

It now appears that this is a possibility.

In the remote future, when people remember the history of the mid-twentieth century to the present, all of the great events that seemed so momentous in this period will be milled away, leaving little trace, and only two things that we have overlooked will be seen as more and more important: first, humanity took its first step outside the cradle, and second, humanity then took a step backward. The importance of these two events cannot be overestimated. The year Gagarin went into space, 1961, could well replace the birth of Jesus as the *annus primus* for humanity; but the decline of space exploration after the Apollo moon landings brought humanity more trauma than our exile from the Garden of Eden.

The period from the late 1950s to the early 1970s will go down in the annals as a golden age. Within just three years of the launch of the first human-made satellite, the first cosmonaut went into space, and only seven more years passed before humanity walked on the moon. At the time, people were stirred by large and remote goals, and believed that in ten more years, give or take, humans would reach Mars, and even reaching Jupiter's orbit to land on Europa did not seem like a remote possibility. Not long before, plans had been born for the bold "Project Orion" to surge off into space, using sequentially exploding atomic bombs to propel the spacecraft, which would be able to carry more than ten cosmonauts to the outer planets.

But soon after, the Apollo missions canceled remaining moon landing missions when funding was cut off. Thus, human space exploration was just like a stone thrown upward in Earth's gravity, reaching a zenith, pausing briefly, and then falling dramatically down. The last Apollo mission—the Apollo 17 moon landing, in December 1972—was a significant turning point, for after that, although there would still be space stations and the space shuttle, and there would be more and more human-made satellites with the economic benefits they bring, and there would be probes sent to the outer planets, still, the quality of human ventures into space was quietly changed, with the gaze of space exploration turning away from the starry skies and down to the ground. Prior to Apollo 17, spaceflight was humanity's effort to leave the cradle; after, it was merely to make the cradle more comfortable. Space ventures were brought in line with economics, with it necessary for product to exceed invention, the noble spirit of exploration replaced with the spirit of business. The wings of the human heart were clipped.

Actually, looking back, did humanity really wish to step outside its cradle? The behind-the-scenes impetus to the mid-twentieth-century wave of space exploration was the Cold War. It was the fear of the enemy and the desire to outdo him. It was a political show of force. Humanity never actually thought of space as its future home.

Now, the moon is once again a waste world with no trace of humans. Russian and American plans for planetary passenger flight have one after the other proven to be pipe dreams, and the "glorious plans" of Europe to explore the solar system have been put on hold. Glory seen no longer. If the space shuttles were taken out of service, the Americans who once walked on the moon would even lose the ability to send people into near-Earth orbit.

Why should this be so? The reasons we can think of are none other than technological and economic ones.

First examine the technological reasons. It is undeniable that humanity does not currently have the technology to undertake large-scale development in the solar system. In terms of propulsion technology, the most basic and most crucial thing for spaceflight, humanity is currently still in the stage of chemical propulsion, while large-scale planetary voyages will require nuclear propulsion, which present technology is still distant from. Nuclear-propelled rockets and ships are still only the stuff of science fiction.

And now look at the economic reasons. With present technology, sending a payload into near-Earth orbit incurs an expense equal to the weight of the load in gold; sending it to the moon or other planets would require ten to upward of a hundred times more capital. Before space development can be made productive, all of this investment would reap very little return. The Apollo moon landings, for example, cost 26 billion US dollars (which would value over 100 billion USD as I'm writing this in 2012), but the missions only obtained about two tons of lunar rocks. (Of course, the technological results from the moon landings program in their application to civil use also produced enormous benefits, but these benefits are hard to quantify and so cannot serve as deciding factors in consideration of policy decisions.)

In sum, development in space is a huge risk, economically and technologically. Making space our new home and betting the human future on this huge of a risk is not something governments can accept.

The reasons listed are a strong argument, seemingly irrefutable, and so have determined the present human space policy and led to the decline of space endeavors. But let us examine what humanity is entirely invested in presently, and what is seen as the single greatest enterprise serving the only road to the survival of human civilization: environmental protection.

In technological terms, space voyages and environmental protection seem different in character, with the former being intense, high speed, and adventurous, with connotations of state-of-the-art technology, while the latter is a gentle green public-service activity, one which, though involving technology, doesn't give the impression of being as difficult as the former.

But that is only an impression. The true situation is: If we want to achieve the present targets for environmental protection, the technology needed is more difficult to develop than that for large-scale interplanetary travel.

If we want to protect the environment, we must first understand its patterns on a global scale. But Earth's ecological systems are extremely complex, so even though every field of science has put enormous amounts of research and understanding into every detail of it, on the holistic global scale, present humanity still has not grasped the patterns and laws for either basic science or practical science. For such systems as the operation of the weather, or changes and interactions among animal groups at large scale, what human science knows is very limited.

One could say without exaggeration: Human understanding of the Earth's surface is not as full as our understanding of the moon's surface, and soon may not be as full as our understanding of the surface of Mars.

On the level of action, the technology currently needed for environmental protection—for example, replacing petroleum with renewable energy sources, managing and recycling industrial and urban waste, protecting biological diversity, and protecting and recovering forest coverage—all involve complex technologies, among which many are not necessarily easier to develop than planetary travel within the solar system.

But the major technological challenge to environmental protection is not in this. Now, human society has entered a period of sustainable development, especially in underdeveloped areas, where development speed is at previously unknown highs. These high-speed development zones have a common goal: to achieve the economic levels of the Western countries, and to have the comfortable modernized lives they lead. Today it seems to be a goal within grasp. With current speeds of development, in another half century, most underdeveloped zones, including countries like China and Brazil, will be able to catch up to the West in economic terms.

But people have overlooked this fact: If the whole world lived the kind of lives those in the US and in Europe do, the resources necessary would be equal to four and a half Earths.

Under these circumstances, if we wish to achieve the final targets for environmental protection—avoiding collapse of Earth's ecosystems and bringing the greatest extinction since the Cretaceous period, happening right now, under control—then only reducing pollution and emissions is far from enough. Even if all the targets of the Copenhagen Accord are realized, the Earth's ecological environment will still sink, just like the *Titanic* from the iceberg.

The only hope is to stop development. But development cannot be suppressed. For some countries and regions to laze about, fully enjoying the comforts of modern civilization, while letting other parts of the world stagnate in the poverty of an agricultural society goes against the most basic value of humanity, and will be a nonstarter in policies, as well.

And consider another possibility: sudden changes to the environment caused by nonhuman factors. The Earth's environment has been oscillating; it's just that human civilization has now been around long enough to perceive this. Each oscillation brings massive change to the whole of Earth's environment, and could make Earth uninhabitable for humans. The most recent ice age, for example, ended only ten thousand years ago, and if another one were to begin, the continents would be covered in ice and snow, causing worldwide agricultural collapse and spelling final extinction for modern society with its massive population. And these massive changes to the environment are, in the long term, nearly inevitable, so much so that they could well happen in the near future. In the face of such environmental change, present environmental protection methods are like a cup of water brought to a bonfire.

If human civilization wishes to survive long-term as the environment changes due to both human-made and natural factors, then it must turn from passive environmental protection behaviors to actives ones, adjusting and changing the Earth's environment in an artificial and comprehensive way. For example, many plans have been introduced to slow the greenhouse effect, including solar-powered steamers of large scale on the ocean, to increase cloud cover by spraying evaporated ocean water to high elevations. Or to build an umbrella with a surface area of three million square kilometers at a Lagrange point between Earth and the sun. Each of these plans is a hyperengineering project of historically unprecedented, even God-like, scale, involving superior technology that would be very much at home in science fiction, but whose difficulty is greater than space travel within the solar system.

Besides the technological difficulties, looking at environmental protection from the economic side, we discover that it is also quite similar to space development: both require large amounts of investment, and both will not see clear economic returns in the early period.

But if we compare human investment in environmental protection to investment in space development, the former is an order of magnitude higher. Taking China as an example, the 12th Five-Year Plan has us investing 3 trillion RMB into environmental protection, but we plan to invest only 30 billion or so into space exploration. The plans of other countries are much the same.

The solar system has enormous amounts of resources. Among the eight planets, in the asteroid belt, all the resources necessary for the development of human existence are present in ample amounts, from water to metals to fissile materials for nuclear fusion, such that if we go by the calculation that Earth could at most support a population of 100 billion humans, then the solar system resources could support one hundred thousand Earths.

Now, we face this fact: Humanity has abandoned those hundred thousand Earths in space, and only plans to continue existing on this Earth, and its method for survival will be environmental protection, a venture as difficult and enormous and risky as opening up space for development.

Just as with environmental protection, space development involves technological progress, with space development driving technological progress forward. Before the Apollo program, the US didn't by any means have the technology needed for a moon landing; a large portion of the technology was developed during the course of the project. Nuclear fission technology is already present on Earth, so to realize nuclear propulsion in space presents no insurmountable obstacles. And although controlled nuclear fusion has not yet been realized, the obstacles are only technological, not theoretical.

We have to face facts like this: In the ships that made it to the moon forty years ago, the power of the guidance and control computers was only the equivalent of one-thousandth of today's iPhone 4.

Space development will closely resemble the Age of Discovery, involving long-distance voyages to unknown worlds, to open up space for human existence and to have better lives. The Age of Discovery began when Columbus arrived in the New World. The voyages of Columbus obtained the support of Queen Isabella of Spain (or more accurately, she was Queen of Castile, for at that time independent Spain did not exist). The queen herself was hard-pressed to supply this fleet, with some saying she pawned her own jewels to help Columbus supply his voyage. Today's facts show that this was a very smart, if risky, investment, to such an extent that some say world history begins from 1500, because it was only from that time that people knew what the whole world looked like.

Now, humans are right at the eve of a second Age of Discovery. We are now much more fortunate than Columbus. Columbus could not see the New World he sought; after sailing many days on the Atlantic Ocean, he saw no land. At this time, he must have been filled with doubt. But the new world we want to survey can be seen by merely lifting our heads. It's just that there is now no one to put up the money.

Perhaps, if we consider human civilization as a whole, it is just like an individual human baby, unable to ever leave its cradle without the help of its parents.

But in the cosmic perspective, Earth's civilization has no parents. Humanity is an orphan in the universe, so we have to look out for ourselves.

ON FINISHING *DEATH'S END,* THE LAST BOOK IN THE REMEMBRANCE OF EARTH'S PAST TRILOGY

TRANSLATED BY HENRY ZHANG

Written September 2, 2010, at Niangzi Pass
First published on the author's Sina blog

The Remembrance of Earth's Past trilogy is now finished. At 880,000 characters, it's a real doorstop.

Recently, I've been getting constant emails, texts, and calls asking me to hurry up with the third book; after a while, I started feeling a bit like the poor tenant farmer, Yang Bailao, from *The White-Haired Girl*, whose ears ring constantly with his landlord's cries: "Cixin, if you can't pay me back by the end of the year, we'll use your daughter as collateral."

All things considered, I think I finished the book quite quickly. The second installment, *The Dark Forest*, was published in 2008; for external reasons, I wasn't able to write for the entire following year. I finished *Death's End* in around a year. Given the one-year hiatus, the book was done very quickly. To really do justice to all 360,000 words of it, I would have really needed three or four years.

We are always clamoring about quality goods—but how are quality goods produced? When it comes to novels, you need time. Of course, there are savants who can write a classic with their eyes closed, but they come around only once in a blue moon. Ordinary authors, like me, need a lot more time to finish our stories; we need to build our worlds, one brick at a time, and engage in a slow, extended dialogue with ourselves.

But even without reader pressure, I wouldn't wait three or four years to finish a novel. The drive for quick gratification rules the day, and I am not immune from its strictures. Authors that can endure such loneliness are extremely rare.

Another reason for the speed is my own sense of crisis. I feel as if my creative output is a tour of my imaginary worlds. I've led this tour group around for ten years, but we haven't even seen half of the scenery, to say nothing of new sites that are opening up. This makes me anxious, because I know the unexpected could happen at any moment; a flood could cut us off, or our bus could be taken hostage. As an avid reader of science fiction, I know my fears aren't groundless.

Of all the unexpected things that might interrupt Chinese science fiction's development, social unrest has to be the most worrying. I once told readers at a conference that science fiction is the product of leisurely and carefree minds. No one agreed, but I was telling the truth. Only when our lives are stable and quiet can we allow the universe's catastrophes to fascinate and awe us. If we already live in an environment full of danger, then science fiction won't interest us. In fact, two of the last three bursts of creative progress that Chinese science fiction underwent were cut short by social unrest, which is lethal to the genre. I hope these are just a science fiction writer's empty worries. I hope that our time of peace and prosperity continues—it would be wonderful for science fiction.

But whatever happens, we ought to pick up our pace as we travel through the land of science fiction. In this new period of life, we ought to be hedonists. To quote *Death's End*: "A moment here; eons there."

THE BATTLE BETWEEN SCI-FI AND FANTASY

TRANSLATED BY ADAM LANPHIER

Written March 5, 2002, at Niangzi Pass
First published in *Science Fiction World*, 2002, no. 5

Last year on Tsinghua's SMTH BBS,* I saw an interesting discussion on this topic: If the worlds of science and magic went to war, which would prevail? The initial consensus was that magic is the stronger force. As one BBSer said, "Try to nuke me, and I'll just ride off on my broomstick." But look closer, and you'll see that's not how it would happen. Why would you run, after all? You'd run because in the world of magic, there aren't any weapons to match a thermonuclear bomb. There's Sun Wukong's Gold-Banded Staff of Compliance in the East, and Zeus with his thunderbolts in the West—but in terms of power, neither of these weapons is in the same league as a human-made twenty-megaton nuclear bomb. Besides, even your broomstick may not save you. The broomsticks in Harry Potter don't seem to go much faster than an Apache helicopter, which isn't fast enough to escape the blast radius of a nuclear bomb.

Here's another obvious imbalance: The world of science sticks to reality, whereas the world of magic is fictional. In reality, brooms can't fly, enchant them as you will, whereas twenty-megaton thermonuclear warheads really do exist. In fact, most of the real artifacts of science have already matched or exceeded what's been imagined in myth: the TV in your house, for instance, or the computer on your desk, or the cell phone in your pocket—the list goes on. What would happen if we used the *fiction* of science fiction to counter the fantasies of magic? An antimatter bomb as big as the Golden Apple in Helen's hand would suffice to sink Mount Olympus in all its glory to the bottom of the sea forever. A slightly larger version of this sci-fi weapon could, in a single strike, boil the oceans dry, or shatter the Earth. A bit bigger still, and it could vaporize the entire magical universe in a powerful beam of light. The world of fantasy and myth isn't really that large. The universe, as depicted in Eastern and Western mythology alike, is hardly ever larger than two astronomical units in radius. The notion of a light-year could never have made it into a myth because such a scale is beyond the capacity of

....

* An online forum (BBS) of Tsinghua University, influential in the early days of the internet in China.

the mythological imagination. The most magnificent deities of the world of magic are dwarfed by the stars of the world of sci-fi, and its most terrible demons pale in comparison to the sci-fi world's black holes.

The brawl between science and magic has been underway for quite some time, within the confines of fantasy literature. Among its more extreme belligerents, there's Bighorn,[†] who clamors for the overthrow of hard science fiction—and I, for my part, have fiercely advocated for the separation of science fiction from literature. We've both been roundly lambasted as a result. That's just how people express themselves online; when Yao Haijun requested that I write this article, he asserted that he "welcome[s] radical views, as long as they're clear," and said that I "don't have to consider every facet of the issue." This is precisely how people talk online—if they didn't, no one would listen. However, we know very well that these extreme views of ours are neither accurate nor reasonable. The truth is that sci-fi and fantasy have many more similarities than differences. They have the same goal: both strive to create ethereal, free worlds of the imagination from which readers can derive the shocks and delights of beauty. (Personally, I've never thought it's sci-fi's job to represent reality or human nature.) The only difference between the two is the source of their imaginings.

Fantasy has been around since antiquity, and there's been so much of it. The years have taken their toll and depleted some of its imaginative power. The rapid progress of science, on the other hand, constantly infuses fresh blood into the science-fictional imagination. The worlds described in today's sci-fi are entirely different from those of a few decades ago, whereas today's fantasy worlds aren't so different from those of the Middle Ages. What's more, the imaginings that science enables are far more capacious and abundant than fantasy's. Without science, talk of distances like 15 billion light-years or 10^{-30} millimeters would be nothing but the ravings of a madman. It was science that introduced such notions into the realm of the imagination, expanding by countless times the scale of what humanity can conceive. Given the circumstances, why would fantasy reject science?

There's another very important reason that fantasy needs science:

....

† A pseudonym of the author Pan Haitian.

We tend to imagine that readers of fantasy recognize that what they're reading is make-believe, which is certainly true today, but wasn't necessarily so in ancient times. People of ages past regarded fantasies and myths as nothing less than fact. Back then, the real world and the world of magic were mixed together as an inseparable whole, and a large part of the appeal of magical fantasy was its perceived realism. Now, its sense of realism is gone for good, which is why modernity can produce only fairy tales, never myths. When readers know a story won't and, indeed, couldn't happen, that story's power to shock is greatly diminished. However, science fiction is able to provide that sense of realism, which makes the advent of modern myths possible, and may even prove able to bring us back to an era in which reality and mythology are fused.

As to the state of sci-fi and fantasy in movies, I think what we're seeing now, in the late nineties and early 2000s, is a mere market fluctuation. A thorough look at the history of cinema shows that fantasy films haven't enjoyed a significant advantage over sci-fi films. After the glut of sci-fi blockbusters we had some time ago, moviegoers naturally wanted to see something different. This by no means implies fantasy's victory over sci-fi. In truth, fantasy and sci-fi aren't even at odds—elements of science fiction will come increasingly to permeate fantasy, and sci-fi may follow fantasy's excellent model and learn the modes of expression it uses to engage readers and enhance its readability.

In summary, all of us should stick to our sci-fi visions and continue expressing them online, in language as pungent as mustard. And the sci-fi community as a whole should maintain a tolerant stance toward different genres (including fantasy) and adopt what's best in them. This is how we'll usher in a new spring for sci-fi and fantasy literature alike, so that their hundred blossoms will bloom.

THE "CHURCH" OF SCI-FI

On Depictions of the Universe in Science Fiction

TRANSLATED BY ADAM LANPHIER

Written December 20, 1999, at Niangzi Pass
First published on February 22, 2001, on the "Science Fiction" message board of Tsinghua University's SMTH BBS

There are many things that current Chinese science fiction lacks, among which is one thing that, despite its extreme importance, has never been noticed or mentioned.

Chinese science fiction lacks religious feeling.

I'll start off by saying that I'm a committed atheist; we know that science and religion are often incompatible. One would think sci-fi and religion ought to be, as well. However, there are scholars who believe that the reason modern natural sciences were born in the West has something to do with the deep religiosity of Western culture. Even a tome too heavy to lift wouldn't be able to get to the bottom of that topic, so I won't try to explore it in any detail here. Instead, I'll limit my topic to the religious feeling in science fiction.

Mind you, what we're discussing isn't religion, per se, but religious *feeling*. This isn't the feeling someone has toward God—it's atheistic, and not in the complicated way of Spinoza or whomever. The religious feeling of science fiction is a deep sense of awe at the great mysteries of the universe.

Consider the two passages below, both of which are the sort of narrative that can be found in many domestic sci-fi stories. The first describes an interplanetary police chase:

> *The police ship swept past planet after planet in hot pursuit of the smuggler craft. The smugglers' captain carefully observed the terrain of each planet they passed, desperate to find one where they could land and stage a showdown with their pursuers. None presented itself, however, and he was left glancing back at the police ship, which was steadily gaining on them, gritting his teeth, and flying onward.*

The second describes a head-on encounter between two giant interstellar ships traveling at a substantial fraction of the speed of light:

"They just passed straight by us!" shouted the navigator; hearing this, the pilot pulled back hard on the ship's steering lever, yawing the Starship XX into a wingover to reverse its course, and took off in pursuit.

The first gives the impression that the universe isn't much bigger than a small town in a police movie, and that planets are like little shops on one of its roads; the second makes the reader feel as if an interstellar spacecraft flying at near-light speed handles more or less like a cab on the street. Passages like these reveal an author who is insensible to the grandeur of the universe. Such scenes can be used to positive effect, like in Sheckley's *The Alternative Detective*. This sort of fiction is allegorical; it uses the universe merely as a tool to develop its plots. The main appeal of science fiction, however, lies elsewhere.

A huge, cosmic craft, flying through the darkness and silence of space toward a distant target, accelerates for two millennia, maintains cruising speed for three, then decelerates for two. Generations of humanity are born and die aboard. The Earth has become a dim, vague, prehistoric dream; onboard archaeologists have been unable to find anything that might confirm its existence among the remains of the ship's tumultuous history. Their remote destination, too, has become like a myth: a religious vision, passed down for thousands of years. Generation upon generation of people who can't figure out where they came from; generation upon generation of people who don't know where they're going. Most people believe that the ship is an eternal world, that it has existed and will exist forever. Only a few wise people are firm in their belief that the Destination exists. Day and night, they peer out ahead of the ship, into the limitless depth of the cosmic abyss . . .

This is the theme of a number of works of Western sci-fi. What do you get a feel for when you read such a passage? The depth and vastness of space? The brevity of human life? It may give you a glimpse through God's eyes, a universal vantage from which to look down on all human history, and you're overcome by the realization that our civilization is but a tiny grain of sand in the desert of cosmic space-time.

One may think that the faster-than-light travel and space-time-leap tech of sci-fi would surely make the universe feel smaller, just as airplanes and modern communications have made the Earth smaller. This is true. If faster-than-light technology is truly possible, then maybe one day, the universe will feel no larger than a village to humankind, much like the "global village" of today. However, we're talking about fiction. Which of the following two novels would you rather read: a story about Columbus on the vast Atlantic Ocean, terrified and faint of hope as he seeks out the New World of his dreams, or the story of a corporate employee's flight from Paris to New York for work?

What's more, the Earth has not, in fact, shrunk. Its vast continents and oceans still exist; modern people still traverse the land by foot and organize the America's Cup regatta, experiencing something of the romance and excitement their distant ancestors did as they trekked across the planet's surface. Most people today have no opportunity even to leave the atmosphere. As such, there is no point for sci-fi to shrink the universe into a village. More importantly, even in the age of faster-than-light travel, the universe as a whole will remain full of great mystery and shocking phenomena.

In "Father to the Stars," Frederik Pohl tells the story of a billionaire who devotes his life and fortune to constructing dozens of spaceships powered by conventional rocket engines. They take off toward open space with tens of thousands of people on board in hopes of expanding humanity's Lebensraum. Decades after they depart, science on Earth makes faster-than-light spaceships a reality, and the protagonist, already an old man, boards one. They catch up with the ships that had departed decades prior in a mere one or two days, turning the protagonist's life's work and the lives of the tens of thousands of pioneers aboard the other ships into a meaningless tragedy. In this story, Pohl uses the contrast between two forms of technology to impart to the reader, in equal measure, a sense of the vastness of space, of the tragedy of the pioneers, and of the remorselessness of fate.

The finest portrayal of space-time jumps in science fiction appears in Arthur C. Clarke's *2001: A Space Odyssey*. The fear, loneliness, and awe that humankind displays for the mysterious universe in that novel leaves an indelible mark on the reader. It's unforgettable. I remember finishing it on a winter night twenty years ago and walking outside to look up at the night sky. I suddenly felt as if everything around me had disappeared, that the ground beneath my feet had become a snow-white, geometric plane that extended into infinity—and that there on that infinite, two-dimensional plane, beneath the resplendent stars, stood I alone, face-to-face with a great mystery beyond the ability of the human mind to comprehend. Ever since then, the stars at night have looked different to me. It felt as if I'd left my pond and seen the ocean. That experience gave me a deep appreciation for the power of science fiction.

In our harried, pragmatic modern world, most people are blinkered by society and practicality. People rarely look up at space. I once asked fifteen people whether the moon is ever visible during the day. One wasn't sure; the other fourteen were quite certain it's not. Modern society also makes its inhabitants numb to numbers. No one has seriously imagined (I mean *imagined*, not calculated) how long a light-year really is, and deep in most people's minds, there's the notion that fifteen billion light-years (i.e., the measure of the universe) is about the same distance as fifteen billion kilometers. Numbness to the universe is pervasive in society.

It is science fiction's mission to broaden and deepen people's minds. If someone on the way home from work at night pauses to look thoughtfully up at the stars for a while because of a sci-fi story they've read, then that work is a great success. Unfortunately, our current sci-fi is also benumbed to a considerable extent, and I see two possible reasons.

The first is conceptual. There's an idea that sci-fi, like mainstream literature, is about relationships between people. This idea reduces the universe to nothing but a prop, a set piece, a supporting role. It cannot be denied that this idea has given rise to many excellent works, but sci-fi is at its strongest and most charming when it depicts the relationship between people and the universe. In sci-fi, the universe itself should be a protagonist, as much as any of its characters. The two sequels to *2001: A Space Odyssey*—*2010: Odyssey Two* and *2061: Odyssey Three*—didn't resonate as deeply because the author shifted their focus to the various relationships between people within society, which undermined the mystery and ethereality of the universe as established in *2001*.

Second, grokking the universe is no easy thing. When you stand on the roof of a tall building, you feel like you're on top of something;

when you're in a hot-air balloon at one thousand meters, this feeling is stronger, such that it's dizzying. But when you look down from a passenger plane flying at twenty thousand meters, your sense of height is weakened, and from a space shuttle orbiting the Earth at an altitude of several hundred kilometers, it may take a good deal of imagination to get a feel for how high up you are. From the moon, 300,000 kilometers away, the Earth looks like nothing more than a pretty, blue bauble. Our human faculties have great difficulty making sense of superlarge distances. The vastness of the universe manifests not only in its great size, but in its microscopic detail, and this sort of vastness is even harder for human senses to apprehend. Modern science, meanwhile, has reached such a deep level of thought about our macrocosmos and microcosmos that the universe it portrays isn't merely beyond what we *do* imagine—it's beyond what we *can* imagine. Truly to appreciate the grandeur of the universe and to capture that grandeur in fiction requires a superior imagination and superlative expressive technique, as well as an author with a fairly in-depth understanding of the cutting edge of modern science. This is sci-fi's eternal, enormous struggle—and its most alluring goal.

Yet all of this is predicated on whether an author regards the universe with religious feeling.

A professor of philosophy once said that lesson one for freshmen in his field should consist of a long, hard look late at night at the stars. I think this would be an even more apt first lesson for aspiring writers of sci-fi. It would give them true access to the seed of sci-fi feeling, which they'd find in the deepest part of their being.

The universe, mysterious and grand, is the "God" of science fiction. The "creed" of the "church" of sci-fi is as follows:

Experience the greatness of the Lord; experience the depth of the Lord; record your experiences for the eyes of busy people, that they may share them and themselves experience the greatness and the depth of the Lord, as you have. You and those busy people are thereby blessed alike.

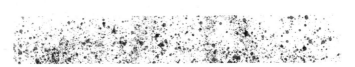

END OF THE MICROCOSMOS

TRANSLATED BY S. QIOUYI LU

Written October 1998, at Niangzi Pass
First published in *Science Fiction World*, 1999, no. 6

Tonight, humanity attempts to split the quark.

The magnificent feat will occur at Lop Nor's eastern nuclear center. The center itself appears to be just an elegant white building in the desert. The enormous accelerator with a perimeter of 150 kilometers, however, is buried in a tunnel deep under the sand. Nearby, a custom-built, 1,000,000,000-watt nuclear power plant generates power for the accelerator. But today's experiment requires even more power, which the grid to the northwest will temporarily supply.

Today, the accelerator will speed particles up to 10^{20} gigaelectron volts, the same amount of energy released during the big bang, when all matter began. With such incredible power, the smallest particle known to humanity will be split, providing answers to the deepest mysteries of the physical world.

There are only a few people in the nuclear center's control room. Among them are two of the most illustrious theoretical physicists on Earth, representing two different approaches to research on the deep structure of matter. Herman Jones, an American, believes that the quark is the smallest particle and cannot be split any further. Meanwhile, Zhang Yi, from China, believes that matter can be infinitely split. Accompanying them are the chief engineer, who supervises operations, and a few journalists. The other workers are in dozens of control rooms deep underground; those in the main control room can see data only once it's been aggregated. The most surprising person present is an old Kazakh shepherd named Dilshat, whose village is located over the accelerator. The physicists tried some of his whole roast lamb yesterday and insisted that he be present today. Their thinking was that this is a moment of truth for physics, a moment of truth for all of humanity—so there should be someone present who has no understanding of physics at all.

The accelerator starts up. On a large monitor, the power curve climbs lazily like a newly awakened earthworm toward a red line showing the critical amount of energy needed to split the quark.

"Why aren't they broadcasting this?" Zhang Yi asks, pointing to a TV set in the corner showing a packed soccer match. Zhang Yi is still wearing the same blue work outfit he had on when he departed from Beijing. It's easy to mistake him for an ordinary handyman.

"Dr. Zhang, we are not the center of the world. If we can get even thirty seconds of airtime on the news after this experiment has concluded, I'd consider that good," the chief engineer replies.

"Ignorant. Unbelievably ignorant," Zhang Yi says, shaking his head.

"But it's a fact of life," Jones says. His entire appearance is dispirited. His hair is long and shaggy, and, from time to time, he takes a flask from his pocket for a swig of alcohol. "Unfortunately, I have the misfortune of not being ignorant. It's hard to live this way." He flashes a sheet of paper to the others. "Sirs, this is my suicide note."

His words startle everyone present.

"After this experiment is over, the physical world will no longer have any mysteries to explore. Within an hour, the entire field of physics will come to an end! I'm here to welcome that time. Ah, physics, what a cruel mistress you are! Once you're exhausted, how can I keep on living?"

Zhang Yi objects.

"People said that back in Newton's day and Einstein's day as well, like Max Born and Stephen Hawking. But the field of physics didn't come to an end then, and it won't come to an end now. Soon you'll see that, once the quark is split, we'll reach another level on the ladder to nowhere. I'm here to welcome the birth of the world!"

"Dr. Zhang, you're simply restating what Mao Zedong believed. He brought up the idea of infinitely divisible matter in the 1950s," Jones shoots back sarcastically.

"You two are too far in your own heads," the chief engineer says, interrupting them. "You can infer that the Earth is round from the differences in solar projections at wells in Egypt and Greece, and you can even calculate the Earth's diameter. But it wasn't until Magellan's trip that people felt inspired. Before, you physicists were all stuck at the bottom of a well. But today, we take a true voyage around the Earth through the microcosmos!"

The energy potential line continues to creep toward the red line. The world outside seems to detect the enormous amount of energy surging deep in the desert: a startled flock of birds takes flight from a grove of tamarisks and pulses through the night sky as distant wolves howl. Finally, the energy potential line crosses the red line. The particles in the accelerator have acquired the energy needed to split the quark, making them the most powerful particles in all of history. The computer leads the energized particles through a ring around the 150 km perimeter of the accelerator, then sends them into a feeder path, where they fly toward their target at close to the speed of light. Under this maximum-energy bombardment, the target bursts with a storm of atomic radiation. Countless sensors stare wide-eyed at the rainstorm. In an instant, they can distinguish the few raindrops that are of a slightly different color. From the combination of colors, the supercomputer can determine whether a quark has been hit, or even whether a quark has been split.

The energized particles continue to be produced and bombard their target. The probability of an accelerated particle hitting a quark is minuscule—no one in the anxious crowd knows how long they'll have to wait.

"Ah, friends from afar," old Dilshat says, breaking the silence. "I was here a dozen years ago when they began building all this. Back then, there were over ten thousand people at the construction site. There were mountains of steel and concrete, and there were hundreds of coils several stories tall. They told me that those were electromagnets. But what I don't understand is this: For the same amount of money, resources, and labor, you could irrigate the desert and fill it with grapes and hami melons. Yet you're doing something no one understands."

"Sheikh Dilshat, we are investigating one of the mysteries of the physical world. This is far more important than anything else!" Zhang Yi says.

"I'm not very knowledgeable, but I do know that all of you with the greatest education in the world seem to be looking for the world's tiniest grain of sand."

Everyone gathered is excited to hear the old Kazakh shepherd's clear description of particle physics.

"Excellent!" Jones shouts once the interpreter is done speaking. "He believes," he said, pointing to Zhang Yi, "that the grain of sand can keep getting smaller. But I believe that nothing can be smaller than that grain of sand. No matter how hard you clobber it, it won't break. Who do you think is correct, sir?"

Old Dilshat shakes his head once the interpreter finishes translating. "I don't know. You don't even know. How can an ordinary person make heads or tails of the outcome of all this?"

"So you remain agnostic?" Zhang Yi asks.

The old shepherd's timeworn eyes sink into deep contemplation.

"The world is truly incomprehensible. Ever since I was young, I've led flocks of sheep through the endless Gobi Desert to look for fresh pastures. There were many nights when I lay out in the wilderness with the sheep and gazed at a sky full of stars. The stars were so thickly dotted together, sparkling like gems, like the jewels in a woman's black hair . . . When the night is young, the sands of the Gobi are still warm beneath you, and the wind sighs with the voice of the desert. In those moments, the world is alive, like a baby deep in slumber. You don't need ears. You simply have to listen with your heart, and you can hear a single sound filling the space between the sky and the earth. That's the sound of Allah. Only Allah can know what the outcome of all creation will be."

At that moment, a buzzer pierces through the air: the signal that a quark has been hit. Everyone turns to the screen to face judgment day. A three-thousand-year-old question will soon be answered.

Data floods the screen. The two physicists immediately realize that something is wrong and shake their heads, perplexed.

The results don't definitively show that the quark has been split, but neither do they show that the quark has remained whole. The data from the experiment is incomprehensible.

Dilshat gives a sudden shout. Of all the people in the room, only he isn't paying attention to the data on the monitor. Instead, he is standing by the window.

"What in the world is going on outside?! Come look!"

"Sheikh Dilshat, please don't disturb us!" the chief engineer snaps, but Dilshat's next words make everyone turn around.

"What . . . what's wrong with the sky?!"

Light streams in through the window. The entire night sky has gone pure white. The people in the main control room rush outside, where, over the limitless Gobi, the once-blue dome of heaven now shines like a sea of milk with a soft white glow, as if the world is now cradled in an eggshell. Once their eyes adapt, the crowd discovers that there are black specks in the white sky. A close inspection of the position of those dots brings them to the brink of madness.

"Subhanallah, those black dots . . . are stars!" old Dilshat shouts, expressing what everyone sees but is too afraid to say: the universe's inverse.

Amid their shock, someone notices that the TV inside is still broadcasting a soccer match. The screen confirms that they're not dreaming: a thousand miles away, the soccer stadium is also shrouded in white light. The tens of thousands of spectators in the stands crane their heads to look up with alarm at the sky.

The chief engineer is the first person to calm down.

"When did this happen?" he asks.

"Just now, when that buzzer sounded," Dilshat replies.

The people gathered fall silent again as they all turn to look at Jones and Zhang Yi, hoping that the two most renowned physicists on Earth since Einstein can make some sense of the nightmare they're in.

Meanwhile, the two physicists are no longer looking at the sky and both have their heads lowered in thought. Zhang Yi is the first to look back up at the blank white universe and let out a long sigh.

"We should have considered this way earlier."

Jones also looks up, meeting Zhang Yi's gaze.

"Yes, this must be the meaning of the supersymmetry equation's variable!"

"What are you talking about?!" the chief engineer shouts.

"Chief Engineer, our voyage around the world is complete!" Zhang Yi declares, smiling.

"You're saying that the experiment caused all this?!"

"Yes indeed!" Jones proclaims as he takes another swig from his flask. "Now Magellan knows that the Earth is round."

"R . . . round?!" the others exclaim as they stare, bewildered, at the two physicists.

"The Earth is round. If you start at any point on its surface and keep going in a straight line, you will return to where you started," Jones explains. "Now, we know the shape of the universe. It's as if we've kept going straight into the microcosmos and reached the end—thus arriving at the macrocosmos. The accelerator pierced through the smallest building block of physics, and the energy impacted the largest building block, turning the entire universe inside out."

"Dr. Jones, you still have something to live for. Physics hasn't come to an end," Zhang Yi says, "it's just begun, like how the field of geography only emerged once we figured out the shape of the Earth. We were all wrong. If I were to pick the analysis that came closest to what actually happened, it would be what Sheikh Dilshat said. Although I don't believe in Allah, the mysteries and secrets of the universe far surpass what we can comprehend."

"I recall that an English science fiction author from the previous century, Arthur C. Clarke, once brought up the idea of the inverse of the universe in a story. Who would have thought that that really exists?"

"But now what do we do?" the chief engineer asks.

"This is good. I'm quite happy living in this inverse universe. It's just as beautiful as the obverse universe, don't you think?" Jones finishes off the rest of the alcohol in his flask. Tipsy, he throws open both arms to embrace the new universe.

"But, look . . ." The chief engineer points to the TV inside the control room. The crowd's agitation and panic is reaching a tipping point into mass hysteria. Surely the rest of the world has fallen into similar chaos.

"Keep bombarding the target," Zhang Yi says to the chief engineer as the computer continues to analyze the results, its bombarding routine suspended.

"Are you crazy?! Who knows what will happen the second time there's a collision with a quark? Maybe it'll cause the collapse of the universe, or even a massive explosion!"

"It won't! What we've seen confirms the theory of supersymmetry. We know what will happen next," Jones says.

The accelerator resumes bombarding the target with supercharged particles. The room waits for those few differently colored raindrops in an atomic storm to appear.

One minute . . . two minutes . . . ten minutes . . .

Curves and data roil through the screen.

Nothing happens.

On the TV, the sea of spectators loses control. Under the pure white sky, people stampede, trampling each other. The picture flickers as the TV's signal goes out, until all that's left is a field of fluttering snow. The universe's sudden change goes beyond all of humanity's understanding, beyond what humanity can bear. The world is on a path to madness.

The buzzer sounds for the second time, signaling a second collision with a quark.

Without warning, the universe returns to its usual state: a pitch-black sky glittering with stars.

"You're doing Allah's work!" old Dilshat says, standing along with everyone else under an intoxicating cosmos on the dunes of the Gobi.

"Yes, our relentless pursuit of the principles of physics has given us the power of God. This is beyond what any of us could have dreamed of," Jones says.

"But we're still only human. Who knows what will happen in the future?" Zhang Yi says.

Slowly, old Dilshat kneels before the heavens.

"Mashallah . . ."

As the stars twinkle in the night sky, an inaudible melody fills the universe.

POETIC SCIENCE FICTION

TRANSLATED BY EMILY XUENI JIN

Written December 22, 2014, at Niangzi Pass
First published in *In the Loop* by Ken Liu, translated by Xiao
Aoran et al., by Sichuan Science and Technology Press in
March 2015

After "The Paper Menagerie" won the Hugo Award for Best Short Story, I wanted to give Ken Liu a set of paper menageries as a present when he visited Beijing. I discovered subsequently that papercraft was really a wonderful art with many surprises. Usually, there isn't any evident correspondence between the paper-folding process and the final product. After a series of complex and inexplicable folds, the paper would take on a seemingly random, shapeless form. However, after a simple inside-out flip, it would suddenly come to life as if touched by magic. Remember the boat with a canopy that your mother taught you how to make when you were a child? That is a classic example. Hence, designing a paper menagerie requires exceptional spatial imagination.

I've been thinking whether mathematical language could be applied to describing papercraft, such as topology. There are many excellent artists in China who make realistic and delicate paper menageries, avant-garde in design. Unfortunately, considering how vulnerable these artworks could be, I could only give Ken Liu smaller and simpler ones that were easier to carry and store. Even so, when I looked at my gifts to him, I could hardly believe that those magnificent shapes were created from merely folding a single piece of paper, no extra cutting needed. I had to control my urge to pull them apart to examine their structure.

Papercraft, to me, is a kind of art that creates beauty from mathematical precision and rationality. The same goes for Ken Liu's science fiction.

The heart of literature is an aesthetic pursuit. We can roughly call this kind of aesthetic by the name of "poeticness." There are two kinds of poeticness in science fiction literature—one of literature's inherent quality, and one of science fiction as a genre.

As a kind of literature, science fiction shares the same playground as its other literary peers, and therefore it should embody literary poeticness, which stems from the depiction of humans. Human-to-human, human-to-society, and human-to-era relationships constitute the main body of literature. In particular, modern literature focuses on the individual's inner world, consciousness, and spirituality, which results in profound and multifaceted expressions of life and humanity—integral to the formation of literary poeticness.

On the other hand, science fiction poeticness comes mainly from the exploration of human-to-technology, human-to-universe, and human-to-nature relationships. Science fiction unfolds in a science-based imagination, with world setting at its core. It uses imagination to construct a world that is surreal but not supernatural. The main subject of literary poeticness in mainstream literature, "characters," is to some extent replaced by "world setting" in science fiction, where environments and species can exist independently as literary figures. The imagination and creativity shown in creating such figures are important components of science fiction poeticness. Science fiction writes the story of real people in surreal world settings. Thus, humanity in a science fiction world is another crucial factor of science fiction poeticness.

Science fiction poeticness is unique to science fiction. Compared to literary poeticness, science fiction poeticness is more closely linked to technology and nature, echoing the rigidness and insurmountability of the laws of nature. Moreover, the aesthetics of science—such as the self-consistency and harmony of logic, symmetry, simplicity, and novelty, which rarely appear in mainstream literature—also constitute a significant part of science fiction poeticness.

Literary poeticness and science fiction poeticness diverge in the way they each tap into aesthetics. Therefore, the two rarely coexist in the same work; they may even have the ability to cancel out each other. Classic science fiction usually excels in one or the other. For instance, traditional Campbellian science fiction such as the works of Arthur C. Clarke and Isaac Asimov embraces science fiction poeticness, whereas the works of Ray Bradbury are classic examples of literary poeticness.

However, Ken Liu, a one-in-a-million science fiction writer, accomplishes the impossible feat of merging literary poeticness and science fiction poeticness.

Ken Liu's works of science fiction are exquisite and unique in their creative core. For example, "The Bookmaking Habits of Select Species" is comprised of a set of wonderful short stories describing the different ways in which different cosmic civilizations record and ingest information, including brains made of flowing water and the reading of information in everything in the universe, including black holes. This story presents a magical picture of cosmic civilizations and cultures that opens our eyes. "The People of Pele," on the other hand, illustrates a kind of crystal-based life-form starkly different from the forms of life we know. The composition and evolution of such a life-form overturn our concepts of biology and greatly expand our imagination of life, and I can safely say that it is the most peculiar imagination of extraterrestrial life I have ever seen.

Science fiction ideas in Ken Liu's other works demonstrate deep reflections on the relationship between human-technology and human-universe. In this regard, "The Countable" is worth our rumination. The story is built upon mathematics; through describing various forms of infinities, it displays a mathematical world that is no longer monotonous, a simple arrangement of strings of numbers, but rather vast and deep as the starry sky. The numbers we encounter via common sense are only the tip of the iceberg. If we reexamine life from this grand mathematical perspective, we will feel that our understanding of life has always been limited and partial. It is through fantastic imagination and profound perspectives that Ken Liu embraces science fiction poeticness.

When describing Ken Liu's works from the perspective of literature, there isn't a word better than "poetic." One can feel a kind of tranquility and softness that rarely appears in science fiction. His writing is like a calm lake in which all the flavors of life in a world of rapidly evolving technology and the sorrows and joys of the universe are reflected. Despite the frustrations, catastrophes, and death involved, the lake is still as placid and smooth as a mirror. This, of course, is not to say that the author is a coldhearted observer who demonstrates no empathy toward the happenings in his stories. We, as readers, can feel how the author has been constantly sympathizing with his surrounding environment. His narrative, so gentle and delicate, filters out the hype and agitation brought about by technology and leaves us with serene poeticness, which can touch the soft spot in our hearts. This kind of gentle, calm poeticness is seen even through "Mono no aware" that depicts an apocalypse and "The Waves" that foreground the grand evolutionary journey of the human race.

When discussing literary poeticness in Ken Liu's works, we cannot avoid his deployment of Asian cultural elements. To clarify here, I do not wish to overemphasize the influence of Chinese and Asian culture on his works—in fact, his work has a strong footing in American culture, and the Asian elements he draws upon are precisely a manifestation of American culture's diversity as well as his own deep-seated knowledge. As the author said in an interview, "My work is *different* from other American writers only in the sense that every American is different from every other American, for such individual difference has been constitutive of what it means to *be* an American since the days of Alexis de Tocqueville's visit." In "All the Flavors," Chinese and American culture, instead of presented as opposites, are each other's complement. The protagonist who came from Chinese history says that they will no longer tell the story of when they were Chinese, but rather the story of how they became an American. Despite this, Asian culture still plays a crucial role in Ken Liu's works that cannot be overlooked. For example, in "Mono no aware," the mentality and behavior of the people facing the apocalypse, the protagonist and his family's sacrifice, are characteristic of Asian culture. Apart from stories like "All the Flavors" and "The Paper Menagerie" that make explicit allusions, elements of Asian culture are rather subtle in his stories, seeping into the works and manifesting as undertones. I believe that the tranquil poeticness, delicateness, and gentleness Ken Liu demonstrates in his works resemble Asian culture profoundly.

Ken Liu's science fiction is a perfect blend of science fiction poeticness and literary poeticness, in which technology is no longer hard and cold or ostracized objects, but rather a part of everyday life and humanity. Before we could notice, our lives are already irreversibly altered and remolded by technology. In this process, no matter what choices are made, life would take on an unfamiliar face, accompanied by unspeakably complex feelings and sensations. In "The Waves," humans evolve from mortals with flesh-and-blood bodies to demigods. In every difficult step they take, however, they continue to preserve the spark of humanity and dignity.

This is not saying that Ken Liu rejects technological progress; rather, he, with a sober eye, sees the complexity of life changed by high technology and the hard choices people are about to face. In "Arc," a story about immortality, a character claims that death giving meaning to life is a lie. Still, the protagonist, tired of immortality, chooses aging and ultimately death to escape from the shackles of time. "Mono no aware" depicts the apocalypse, a common trope in science fiction, like a long lyrical poem. The themes of doom, escape, and sacrifices are submerged in poeticness. "The People of Pele" embodies another kind of poeticness, where the new life of humans in a new world is balanced against the incredible yet artistically beautiful alien life, and tells us that the universe harbors infinite possibilities toward life and living. In "The Message," practically, the sign that the aliens use to mark the radioactive materials is a failure, but the elegance and magnificence it contains is impressive. The most insightful depiction of life is "The Countable": In the face of the mathematical nature of Mother Nature, utterly cognitively incomprehensible to us, our own lives also exist beyond our imagination. The "life" that our rational mind can grapple with is only comprised of a few protruding iceberg tips, leaving the bulk uncountable. A world composed of numbers transcends sense and reason—what a confusing and frightening scene!

To be honest, I did not pay enough attention to Ken Liu's works when I first came across his writing—that was also when I went through a phase of unsettledness and lethargy in reading, where I only skimmed stories for their shock value and thrills. However, things began to change. If every work of science fiction was a piece of music, then as time went on, I found that after all the other tunes have gradually faded out, Ken Liu's melody still persisted, growing more and more distinct every day. I then went to seek all of Ken Liu's works and devoured them. I realized, after reading, that science fiction isn't only about creativity and thrills, but also elegance, profoundness, and poeticness.

On this note, Ken Liu's works, an impeccable integration of science fiction and literary poeticness, are unique and utterly irreplaceable.

CIVILIZATION'S EXPANSION IN REVERSE

TRANSLATED BY ADAM LANPHIER

Written September 14, 2001, at Niangzi Pass
First published in *Science Fiction World*, 2003, no. 2

When the alien civilization that generations have dreamed of, have called out for, have sought—when that civilization finally comes to Earth, humankind may find itself faced with an uncomfortable situation that has never occurred to it, even in its dreams: The aliens might ignore our welcoming, outstretched hands, choosing instead to embrace and converse with the ants.

This raises a question we've never seriously considered:

Who's the Earth's head of household?

If you take it for granted that we are, you'll find you're deluding yourself: It hasn't been much more than a million years since we climbed down from the trees, and the oldest civilization whose legacy we can realistically claim as our own arose just five thousand–odd years ago. Hundreds of millions of years ago, ants were already forging their great empires on each of Earth's ancient continents. Compared to them, we're nothing but homeless orphans who've just wandered into the room and asked for a cup of water. We're nowhere near head-of-household level.

You'll no doubt protest: *That's ancient history! We have civilization, and human civilization is what raises Earth's standing in the universe.*

Yet so far, at least, the evidence hasn't proven that. We think of the Late Cretaceous, with its asteroid impact and the subsequent extinction of most life on Earth, including the dinosaurs, as the most horrific period in the history of life on this planet. What you might not know, however, is that species are going extinct at a much faster rate now, in the Era of Civilization, than they did at the end of the Cretaceous. The most horrific period in the history of life on this planet is *now*! Civilization might be the path of light by which life perpetuates through the generations . . . or it might be a trap, a one-way road to the extinction of all life, ours included.

The defining feature of modern, technological civilization is its tendency toward expansion. Civilization constantly extends its borders, growing in scale as if it were a balloon being blown up, without a thought as to when it will pop.

Consider the Age of Exploration, full of desire and passion at sea. In that short era, European civilization, roused from sleep by the Renaissance, spread like a swarm of locusts to every corner of the globe.

As for what's ahead: If civilization manages to persist, it will by necessity expand in scale indefinitely and become an enormous macrocivilization. Sci-fi writers have offered many vivid depictions of such superscale civilizations. Larry Niven's *Ringworld*, for instance, depicts an enormous structure encircling a star that such a civilization has constructed; in Asimov's Foundation series, humans have spread throughout the whole of the Milky Way; and in Clarke's *2001: A Space Odyssey*, the supercivilization makes use of a hyperspace structure—a thing beyond humanity's capacity ever to understand—that in effect turns the entire universe into their backyard.

But what we're writing is *science* fiction; if we're to make slightly more serious predictions about humanity's ultra-long-range future, we must do so within the parameters of mathematics and the laws of physics. Otherwise, we're not making predictions, we're writing myths.

When a civilization begins expanding throughout the universe, its natural first step is its own star system. As you probably know, the geometric expansion of a biome is a terrifying thing. Imagine that the surface of the Earth is a growth medium, covered in a nutritious colloid: If you put an invisibly small speck of a bacterial culture anywhere on its surface, then went off on your summer holiday, that speck would most likely have covered the whole planet before your break was half over. If human technology advances sufficiently, expansion into the star system will be similar: a storm of humanity, propelled by the unfeeling laws of economics, that sweeps across the entire solar system. You'll realize then that our planetary system is a small place—that even with the metals of Mercury and the asteroid belt, the territories of Venus and Mars, the liquid and solid hydrogen of Jupiter, the materials of Europa and of the rings of Saturn and Uranus, and the methane of Pluto, we still wouldn't have nearly enough resources for our consumption! Humanity would soon face an ecological and existential crisis in the solar system, just as it had on Earth. Civilization's next step would be to expand into extrasolar space, at which point it would bump up against an impenetrable wall: the speed of light.

There is no theoretical or observational proof for the existence of wormholes through space-time, and spatial folding is a fool's errand. Our current theoretical framework doesn't allow anything to exceed the speed of light. As I said earlier, to distinguish our predictions from mere myths, we must abide by this limitation. Indeed, with any means of astronautical propulsion foreseeable at present—fusion power, solar sails, and so on—we'd be hard-pressed to get a substantial interstellar vessel moving at even one-tenth the speed of light. At that speed, a trip to the nearest star and back might take nearly a century; a return trip to a star with significant available resources might take thousands of years, or even longer. Such a time frame would never be tolerable to the fast-growing economy of a technologically advanced society. Therefore, a global civilization of the future would propagate to other stars much as a dandelion spreads its seeds on the wind, which scatters them far apart before they land and grow into new dandelions. They'd have no way to connect with each other, and they'd never be able to reunite as a single entity. If Asimov's Galactic Empire were real, it would be an enormous and unfathomably slow beast—when its brain wanted to move a finger, it would take a million years for the order to get to the finger, and another million for the brain to learn whether the finger did, in fact, move.

From this, we can infer that there is no interstellar macrocivilization in the universe. In other words, unlimited spatial expansion is not a feasible way to advance civilization.

Let's shift our thinking toward the opposite direction. We'll return to our first topic: ants. How have they survived? Why didn't they go extinct like the dinosaurs? One critical factor is their small size. An ecological community with small individual members needs little space and few resources to survive, and as a consequence, it's better at surviving. The space occupied by a single dinosaur that had lain down to nap would, to a city-state of ants, be an immense domain, and what was half a mouthful of meat to a *Tyrannosaurus rex* would be a year's rations for every denizen of an ant metropolis. In nature, taxa whose individual members are small are therefore at a self-evident advantage. Nature itself may have taken note of this: If you look at the most prevalent trends of natural selection, you'll find that as organisms evolve, they tend to shrink.

Shrinking one's scale is tantamount to expanding one's room for living. We might call this the civilization's "expansion in reverse."

In the long run, expansion in reverse may be the only way forward for human civilization. It's a bit more realistic, technology-wise, than breaking the speed-of-light barrier. Humans just need to technologically intervene in their evolution to shrink themselves steadily over time. It is easiest now to envision this being accomplished through genetic engineering. At the rate that technology is developing, it isn't hard to picture human beings one day being able to manipulate genes as if they were compiling a computer program, at which point biology will be capable of miracles that defy the imagination. On Earth today, among mammals with some resemblance to humans, the ones with the smallest bodies are rodents. With genetic engineering, humanity might one day shrink its members down to the size of little white mice, and were we to do so, the world would appear radically different to us. Imagine it: An ordinary two-bedroom house of today would be nothing short of a monumental palace to them! The Earth is *already* an unimaginably vast place to human beings.

This is just how expansion in reverse might begin, the first step toward a true microcivilization. Such a shrinkage would come nowhere near providing for civilization's ultimate development. To create a space vast enough for the supercivilization of the future, humans may have to shrink themselves to the size of bacteria! This sounds like an off-the-wall idea—to realize it would require far more sophisticated technologies than genetic engineering: nanomechanics and others we can't yet imagine—but unlike faster-than-light travel and spatial folding, it at least doesn't violate any of the basic laws of physics as they're presently understood. At the microscopic level, the atoms and their quantum states in a bacterium-sized mass are sufficient in number to store and process all the information that is currently stored and processed in a human brain. Maybe you still think it's an impossible idea, but consider what would happen if you took a Pentium 4 microchip a hundred years into the past and talked about what was stored in that little trifle—it would have seemed like incomprehensible gibberish.

What would a civilization made up of bacterium-sized members look like? How would the world appear to them? Take a second to explore the idea—you'll soon find doing so to be an unusually exhilarating imaginative exercise. Here's one of my humble attempts, taken from my short story "The Micro-Era," which is included in the *Wandering Earth* story collection:

> The Forerunner indulged in the warm bliss of imagination: he could picture the micro-humans' wild joy when they would first see a colossal green blade of grass rising to the heavens. And what about a small meadow? What would a meadow mean to micro-humanity?
>
> An entire grassland! What would a grassland mean? A green cosmos for micro-humanity! And a small brook in the grassland? What a majestic wonder the sight of the brook's clear waters snaking through the grassland would be in the eyes of a micro-human. Earth's leader had said there could be rain soon. If rain fell, there could be a grassland and that brook could spring to life! Then there could certainly be trees! My God, trees!
>
> The Forerunner envisioned a group of micro-human explorers setting out from the roots of a tree, beginning their epic and wondrous journey upward. Every leaf would be a green plain, stretching to the horizon.
>
> There could be butterflies then. Their wings would be like bright clouds, covering the heavens. And birds, their every call angelic trumpets blaring from the heavens.

Scientists, in their speculations about how alien civilizations might behave and the traces they might leave, have historically tended to assume macroscopicity, as in the well-known hypothesis that once a would-be interstellar civilization has reached a certain point in its development, it will by necessity make maximal use of the energy of its home-system star, and as a result, the worlds it lives on will take the form of rings around the star, or even encase the star in its entirety. It follows that by looking for signs of such a star, we may well find an alien civilization. But let's try starting from the microscale as we consider the existence of alien civilizations: Once civilizations have reached a certain point in their development, they will by necessity miniaturize themselves. This is of no help in our search for alien civilizations, but it would explain why we haven't seen any so far. A microscale civilization would inevitably not give off much energy to the outside world (whether it meant to or not), making it more difficult for us to detect it. Imagine an alien race whose members are the size of bacteria—they could be right under your nose, holding their Olympic Games, and you'd have no way to detect their presence.

But miniaturization as such is not the ultimate in civilization's development. It's possible that a supercivilization might, as Clarke describes in *2001: A Space Odyssey*, have "frozen [itself] in a lattice of light." Such civilizations would have entirely transcended the notion of scope; they could shrink to the size of an atom or grow to the size of a galaxy, if they so desired. Speculations about this sort of civilizational apex are showing up more and more in sci-fi. "The Gravity Mine," by Stephen Baxter, is a work from the US that was nominated for the 2001 Hugo Award for Best Short Story, which depicts a human civilization of the distant future comprised of force fields and radiation. Such speculations can even be found in serious scientific thought: *The Last Three Minutes*, a work of popular science by Paul Davies, is a masterful example. To us, however, this sort of civilization seems like a philosophical or even metaphysical subject, and by comparison, the microscopic civilization you found so enigmatic just a moment ago seems much more concrete and tangible.

We can envision another sort of ultimate civilization that, even compared to that ethereal, godlike civilization of force fields, is possessed of grandeur and majesty without peer. This sort is the microscale civilization that goes macroscale in the end. The necessary result of a microcivilization's expansion into the universe is once again to expand to a macrospatial scale, but in a way that's qualitatively different from that of primeval macrocivilizations, those whose members are themselves large. This reexpansion will represent another transcendence: the most glorious symphony that life will compose in the universe! I'll draw a single picture of this sort of civilization and leave the remainder for you to imagine:

A grand fleet of interstellar crafts sail into the solar system. Though each ship is as large as the moon, it's piloted by a mere few thousand bacterium-sized astronauts, who, even if they were gathered together, we'd need a microscope to see.

When it comes to what the future holds for life and civilization in the universe, all our fantasies are feeble indeed.

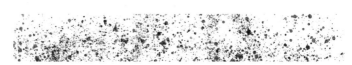

DESTINY

TRANSLATED BY ANDY DUDAK

Written May 11, 2001, at Niangzi Pass
First published in *Science Fiction World Amazing Files*, 2002,
no. 3 (Sundance)

We discovered the asteroid 1,800,000 kilometers from Earth.

It was an irregular ovoid with a diameter of about ten kilometers. It revolved slowly, the many little planes and facets of its surface reflecting sunlight like blinking eyes. Our shipboard computer showed its orbit would intersect with Earth in eighteen days. This massive chunk of space rock would strike near the Gulf of Mexico.

Earth's lookout network should have noticed this a year before, but we hadn't heard anything about it in the news. We contacted Earth, but after the expected five-second lag, our earpieces were still quiet. We tried several more times and received no answer. It was like humanity was in collective shock. We'd exchanged words with Earth only ten minutes before. The radio silence amazed us more than our asteroid discovery.

Twenty days before, Emma and I had chartered this small ship for a space-cruising honeymoon. It was an old ship under traditional propulsion. In this era of space-time jump flights, our snail-slow old-school cutter seemed romantic and sentimental. We had toured synchronously orbiting Space City, then Luna, and then flown more than a million kilometers up-system. The journey had gone smoothly, idyllic as an old pastoral song, but on the eve of our planned return, things took a turn for the abnormal.

There it was, fifty kilometers off our bow, clear against the dark backdrop of space, real as a museum exhibit on black satin, and I was sure this wasn't a nightmare.

"We have to do something," I said.

As always, once I'd issued a call to action, Emma set about planning the details: "We could fire an engine at it, blow it off course."

A computer sim confirmed this was feasible, but it would have to be done within twenty-four minutes. If the planetoid moved beyond that window undisturbed, it would be too late.

We didn't hesitate any longer. We moved to a safe distance of one hundred kilometers from the asteroid, then issued the order to the computer. The engine separated from the tail section of our hull. We watched through a porthole as the cylinder spouted blue flame and headed for the rock. The blaze soon became a radiant little star. We held our breaths watching it collide with that massive boulder floating in space. After the initial flash, an immense fireball erupted from the asteroid, expanding fast, as if a new sun had suddenly instantiated before us, and was coming for us. Just when it seemed the inferno would engulf our ship, the expansion slowed, and suddenly it was shrinking, and then it was gone. There was the asteroid again, its surface marked by the engine detonation, the diameter of the crater at least three thousand meters. Countless points of light were flying out from the asteroid, impact ejecta, among them a fragment that swept past our ship. The computer was determining the asteroid's new trajectory, and we nervously waited.

"Course change successful. The body will not collide with Earth. It will be captured at an orbit of 58,037 kilometers and become an Earth satellite."

Emma and I hugged, overjoyed.

"Think the leasing company will make us pay for that engine?" she asked, half joking.

"Would they dare ask that of humankind's saviors? Besides, we're entitled to proprietary rights on this planetoid. Mineral extraction alone will make us billions!"

With the joy and pride of saviors, we fired the remaining engine and headed for Earth. But once again we got no answers to our hails, leaving us again in suspense. We just couldn't imagine what was going on at home.

Our going was slow on one engine, and the asteroid passed us, soon vanishing in Earth's direction. Emma, who'd been watching its progress on-screen, cried out: "God! Earth! Look at Earth!"

I looked, but at this distance it was baseball-sized, a glittering blue sphere, and I saw nothing strange. Emma pointed at the magnified image on-screen. After a quick scan I began to grow afraid: It was the continents. They'd changed. They looked like nothing I'd ever seen.

We turned to the computer for help, and it responded: "You're seeing the continent shapes and distribution of the Late Cretaceous, including the supercontinent Gondwana."

"The Cretaceous? How . . . long ago was that?"

"Approximately sixty-five million years. But your question may be framed incorrectly. Many signs indicate that the Cretaceous is now."

The computer was right. Now we understood why Earth had gone radio-quiet: Humanity didn't exist yet.

In our home era, space-time jump flights made interstellar travel possible. Every time an interstellar ship jumped, it left behind one or more wormholes, which then drifted in near-Earth space. If an interplanetary ship accidentally entered one, it might be flung instantaneously tens of thousands of light-years, far forward or back in time. Later, improved interstellar ships led to a purge of the spatial dimensions in these left-behind wormholes; that is, they would no longer change your location in space, but might still produce a time jump. Such wormholes were vastly less dangerous. If you accidentally went through one, all you had to do was retrace your route and go back through the other way, returning to the exact moment you left.

We'd gone through such a time-oriented wormhole without sensing it at all.

Accidental time-hole jumps occurred from time to time, but the backward-jumping ships always returned, among them a planet-mining ship that found itself in the Cambrian period. The astronauts saw an Earth glowing dark red, without oceans, the dry land flowing with magma.

Meanwhile, the forward-jumping ships never returned, a cause for great optimism about the future.

But Earth governments were still most focused on the backward jumps. There were strict ordinances. If you happened into a wormhole, by law you had to return. If you couldn't return because of wormhole drift (the probability of this was very low), you had to get a sufficient distance from Earth and then self-destruct, to avoid changing Earth history.

"God," Emma cried, "what have we done?"

My spirits were also low. In a flash, we'd gone from saviors to devils.

"Don't worry, dear," I consoled, "not every little disturbance triggers a butterfly effect."

"Little disturbance? That's what you call what we did?" She remembered something and asked the computer, "This is the Cretaceous?"

The computer replied in the affirmative. We both understood. What we'd nudged off course was none other than that fateful asteroid, the dinosaur killer.

After a long silence, Emma said, "Let's go back."

We promptly turned the ship around and carefully sped back along our original course.

"But what are we returning to?" I sighed. "A trial?"

"Ideally. If humanity still exists, never mind judges, we can die easy."

Smiling, I shook my head. "You worry too much, Emma. Think about it. Why did humans come out ahead of other species? Why not ants? Or dolphins, or other such animals? They have societies, intelligence . . . but their degree of civilization doesn't measure up to our scraps. Opportunities for species evolution are fair and impartial."

"Okay then, why?"

"Because humanity is the spirit, the soul, of all living things. The cosmos chose us. Look how far our civilization has come. This confidence is warranted! The world we go back to might be changed somewhat, but humanity will exist, and so will human civilization!"

Emma smiled a bit. "I forgot what a believer in human selection theory you are." She made a sign of the cross over her chest. "I can only hope you're right."

When we passed back through the wormhole, it felt like the cosmos vanished and reappeared. The process was very short. It was like space blinked, and that was that. No wonder we hadn't noticed the first time through. During the instant of passage, Earth's silence was replaced by a clamor of EM signals, but our excitement turned immediately to disappointment. The signals seemed to be nothing but muffled bursts of chirps and hoots. Neither we nor the computer could interpret them. We shouted at Earth and still got no answer. Once again, we saw Earth on the screen, the continents now restored to their familiar arrangement, and this at least let me breathe and relax for a moment. If there really had been a butterfly effect, at least it hadn't inverted heaven and earth.

Our little ship flew on its remaining engine toward Earth. We entered low Earth orbit two days later and had just enough fuel left for descent. We splashed down in the Pacific, near Australia, and the ship quickly began to sink. We had to repair to a small life raft, and then we were adrift. It was the wee hours of the morning. The sun hadn't risen. I looked around and the ocean seemed like the same old ocean, the sky the familiar sky. The world seemed unchanged.

After drifting half an hour, we saw a large vessel in the distance. We shot a signal flare and the ship came speedily toward us.

"Humanity!" Emma yelled, her eyes shining with excited tears. "It really still exists!"

"I said so, didn't I? Humans are the soul of all living things. We're destined to have the peak civilization."

"But this world isn't the one we set out from." She was afraid again. "Look at that ship. I don't think humans have entered the technological era yet."

The ship appeared quite ancient, nothing like the vessels of our modern world. But that didn't mean this world was technologically backward. I noticed the ship had no sails and wondered about its motive power.

It sped toward us and then came to a halt. A rope ladder came down the side. Emma and I climbed up. The crew were tanned and weathered-looking and dressed in rough gray-green clothes. I addressed them but no one responded; then one of them motioned for us to follow him.

We went up a long flight of steps, ascending the ship's central tower-like structure, which commanded a view of the whole vessel. Our guide presented us to a powerfully built, silver-bearded old man, and said something to us. We didn't understand, but the computer I wore on my chest did. It said: "Their tongue is similar to ancient Latin, with some differences. The sentence may be understood as . . . *This is our captain.*"

The captain also spoke to us, and the computer translated: "You two were drifting alone on the sea. Such bravery! Aren't you afraid of getting devoured?"

"Devoured?" I said, the computer translating and amplifying my words. "By what?"

The captain gestured at the ocean. By now the sun had risen, and a thin morning fog on the sea's surface scattered golden sunlight. The water, tranquil until moments before, now surged with waves, which soon broke, and an immense monster breached the surface. Then came another, and amid the roaring water, a whole pod of the beasts soon emerged. Emma and I finally understood the consequences of what we'd done 65 million years before.

Dinosaurs had never gone extinct.

One came toward the ship, halting alongside, its immense body like a frightful mountain peak, and we were in its vast shadow. I saw black, crisscrossing blood vessels under the gray, satiny skin, like vines and tendrils entangling the great gray summit. The dinosaur's massive neck extended forward, suspending the huge head above us, and seawater came down like torrential rain, flooding the deck. A pair of colossal eyes watched us fixedly. Our blood almost congealed under that grim, cold gaze. Emma pressed against me, shuddering from head to toe.

"Don't be afraid," the captain said. "It can't hurt anyone. This is a zoo."

Sure enough, the dinosaur watched us for a while, then turned and swam away, its wake surging against the side of the ship and rocking it. We spotted another big ship like ours, far off upon the sea, with two dinosaurs swimming before it.

"You've domesticated dinosaurs?" Emma said. "Amazing!"

I too was astonished. "We thought dinosaurs would pose a threat to human evolution. Now we see they've only made human civilization stronger!"

Emma nodded. "Exactly! As beasts of burden they're clearly stronger than oxen or horses. I guess they could move a small mountain without much effort! Darling, you really were right. Humans are the soul of all living things. From now on, I'm a confirmed believer in human selection theory!"

The computer translated our words, and the captain watched us, seemingly baffled. "This is a zoo," he said. "They don't harm people."

Just then I made another surprising discovery: a vision of towering, pillar-like structures on the horizon, their altitude truly shocking. A cloud bank floated about halfway up the immense columns. We were like ants looking at a titanic forest. I asked the captain what it was.

"A building complex," the captain said, indifferent. "A coastal sky-scraper complex."

"God!" Emma cried. "How tall are they?"

"Some ten thousand of you."

"A building over ten thousand meters high?" I said. "That would mean, what, several thousand floors?"

The captain shook his head. "A hundred or so."

"Each level a hundred meters high?" Emma exclaimed. "What a grand palace!"

"A grand civilization," I said. "A grand *human* civilization!"

"Those structures were built by the tourists," the captain said.

"Tourists?" I said. "Ah yes, you said this is a zoo, but . . . tourists? You lot are obviously not tourists."

"It's early," Emma said. "Maybe the zoo is still closed?"

The captain stared at us in amazement, then turned to look at the distant swimming dinosaurs. This confused us, gave us pause, as did the slow, unsophisticated manner of these humans before us.

A howling chorus erupted from the pod of dinosaurs. The clamor was familiar: we'd heard it in space, coming from Earth via radio. We again marveled at the ten-thousand-meter buildings on the horizon, before a revelation burst in my mind like a thunderclap. At my side, Emma cried out in dismay and fell to the deck, as if suddenly paralyzed.

She surely understood now, like I did.

The cosmos had not chosen humanity after all. In the old timeline, humans had created the apex civilization on Earth, but that had been a one-time and accidental chance. In our human conceit, we'd taken the accidental for the inevitable. Now nature had tossed the evolutionary coin again, and it had come up tails instead of heads.

We were indeed in a zoo, but the dinosaurs were the tourists.

My legs went weak. I fell down and sat with Emma on the deck. The world before our eyes was a dark abyss. We heard the computer translation of the captain's words:

"You two are rather exquisite looking. I think it will be okay if you stay with us. Both of you will be approved as ornamental humans."

"Ornamental humans?" I asked, stupefied. The world gradually came back into focus. There was the grand city on the horizon.

"No," Emma muttered, "I want to go ashore . . ."

"Are you mad?" the captain said. "Ashore, you would become a food human!"

"A . . . food human?"

"Food for *them*. Several thousand food humans are supplied to that city every day! Only in the zoo can you be an ornamental, saved from being food. All humans aspire to this."

The world seemed suddenly changed into a grim, sinister meat locker. We were thoroughly desperate, and despairing. I was ready to give up on survival, had already begun to plan how to end my life, when Emma pointed skyward and cried, "Look!"

And there it was, a shining celestial body. It had, until a moment before, been hiding in the morning sun's brilliance. Now we could see it clearly. It was orbiting fast, fast enough for us to perceive it moving. Watching carefully, I could see it wasn't just a point of light, but a mass with definite shape.

"The Demon Star," the captain said. "A tourist scientist says they are researching it. They say it was on a collision course with Earth, long ago, and their Savior used a violent explosion to push it away. The tourists claim their ancestors thus avoided extinction. They say there is a crater from this fateful explosion still on the Demon Star's surface. Look there . . ." The captain pointed toward the distant city, at its tallest tower. "That is the cathedral. The tourists worship their Savior inside."

"Do you know where we come from?" I said. I couldn't help it.

The captain shook his head. He wasn't interested. Curiosity belonged to the apex species, it seemed. These humans didn't have it. They might as well have been ants or bees.

"Evolutionary fate is callous," I said to Emma, to myself, maybe even to those other humans who could never understand me. "Callous and unfeeling. Indifferent. Humanity once enjoyed good fortune. We were lucky and we didn't even know it. But now . . . well, we're not ants or bees, not yet. We still have opportunities, and we should seize them, and not yield to fate."

"You're right," Emma said. "We've changed history once, if unintentionally. Why not change it again?"

I looked at the distant, towering cathedral, then pointed at the pod of dinosaurs and asked the captain, "Those . . . tourists. They must really worship their Savior, right?"

The captain nodded. "As far as they are concerned, the Savior is supreme."

Emma and I connected to the computer through our retinal screens. We retrieved the ship's flight files, finding every detail of the course alteration 65 million years ago, including data and images. Everything had been recorded.

"Can you speak their language?" Emma asked the captain, who nodded.

"Excellent," I said. "Tell them we are the Saviors who pushed away the Demon Star. Tell them we have irrefutable proof."

The captain and his crew stared at us, dumbfounded.

"Quickly, if you don't mind! Later I'll tell you the other story of humanity, but for now, please relay our message to the tourists, and be quick about it!"

The captain cupped his hands around his mouth and yelled in the dinosaurs' direction. His voice was tenuous and weak compared with their howls. It was hard to believe he was speaking their language.

But the pod of dinosaurs immediately stopped playing. They turned their heads toward us as one, and as one they swam toward our big ship.

THE DARK FOREST THEORY

TRANSLATED BY EMILY JIN

Written January 2015, at Niangzi Pass
First published in *Shanxi Literature*, 2015, no. 2

As an old science fiction fan (I won't hesitate to identify myself as someone who belongs to the first generation of science fiction fandom in China), I have always believed that a multitude of intelligent beings and civilizations exist in the universe. If some of these civilizations know about the existence of other civilizations and communicate with one another, then it is highly possible that a cosmic society of civilizations exists. What does this society look like? What are the relationships between these cosmic civilizations? I have long been fascinated with such questions.

Chinese science fiction usually holds a rose-tinted view of extraterrestrial civilizations. Therefore, for the sake of being rebellious, I decided to try and imagine the worst universe possible.

The only reference in reality for the study of cosmic civilized societies is the human society itself. There are different civilizations on Earth, each of which is extremely complex; the interactions between those civilizations are also intricate and convoluted, with countless political, economic, and cultural factors acting in between. Therefore, it is difficult to reach a clear conclusion of how a cosmic civilized society would look if we merely balance it against the human society.

One day, however, I was inspired by a soccer match—my first live match, at the Workers' Stadium in Beijing, China vs. Sampdoria. At the time, I had just started working, and could only afford the cheapest tickets. Sitting in the very last row, I gazed down at the stadium far below. The distance had made the complex technical moves of the players a blur. All I could see was an ever-evolving matrix of twenty-three dots (one special dot being the soccer ball). Even Gullit, the star of the night, was nothing but a moving dot to me. While I regretted not bringing my binoculars, I also felt that this soccer match displayed a clear-cut mathematical structure due to the concealment of details.

I suddenly realized that the scene before my eyes was exactly what the stars looked like.

The distance between stars conceals the complex inner structure of each civilized world. In the eyes of observers like us, alien civilizations are merely dots of light; the complexities and nuances of each civilization are represented as each dot's limited parameters and variables. Therefore, the cosmic society of civilizations should also resemble a mathematical structure.

If we are to examine the cosmic society of civilizations through this perspective, we need to first establish our footing with an axiomatic system on which to base our deductions. The axioms I propose are as follows:

First: Survival is the primary need of civilization.

Second: Civilization continuously grows and expands, but the total matter in the universe remains constant.

The first axiom should be solid. The latter half of the second axiom has not yet been proved by cosmology. However, if I only use these two axioms in science fiction as a part of worldbuilding, I believe that they should make logical sense.

Then, based on facts, we can make three major deductions:

Firstly, mutual communication and understanding between cosmic civilizations is extremely difficult, and it is basically impossible to tell whether the civilization we are interacting with is well-intentioned or malicious. This is because:

a) Given current known laws of physics, communication between stars comes with an extensive time lag due to the sheer distance.

b) The enormous biological difference contributes to the communicational hindrance. On Earth, biological beings are classified into kingdom, phylum, class, order, family, genus, and species. The higher up on the hierarchy, the more different the organisms. It is utterly impossible for humans and organisms of different genus to understand each other. Putting this in the scale of the cosmos, if we take into account the existence of non-carbon-based organisms, then it is very possible for the difference between aliens and humans to exceed the level of kingdom.

Secondly, technological explosion. It took one hundred thousand years for humans to advance from the Stone Age to the Agricultural Age, yet only a mere two hundred years to move from the Steam Age into the Information Age. Any civilized world could welcome technological explosion at any given moment. Therefore, even baby civilizations in their primitive stages or budding civilizations could be dangerous.

Thirdly, detection is reversible. I derived this speculation from "the principle of optical path reversibility" in optics. In the universe, if one civilization could detect the existence of another, then sooner or later, the reverse would happen.

We can make a set of simple deductions based on my proposed axioms and speculations, establishing a sample model of a cosmic civilized society. I have delineated the process of my deduction in *The Dark Forest*, book 2 of the Three-Body Problem series. As I had hoped, I arrived at the worst universe possible. As the title reveals, my universe is unbelievably dark, and only one kind of relationship exists between civilizations: The moment one civilization discovers another, it would do anything to destroy it. This relationship has nothing to do with the ethical values of the civilizations themselves; as long as the two axioms that I had previously proposed hold true, "destroy others" would be an inevitable code of conduct for all cosmic civilizations. My Chinese readers coined my conclusion the "Dark Forest theory."

My conclusion, on the other hand, is a possible explanation for the Fermi paradox—possibly the darkest: If any civilization in the universe revealed its existence, it would be wiped out within a blink of an eye. Therefore, our universe is utterly silent.

Of course, my speculation is only one possibility out of many that science fiction could offer. At present, we are still unable to confirm or dispel the Dark Forest theory in the face of the uncanny silence of the universe.

Science fiction is fundamentally a literature of speculation. It lists a multitude of possibilities for its readers to enjoy and ponder over, and the most fascinating ones are usually the most unlikely ones. However, in this magical universe, any impossibility may become a reality. As some astrophysicists have posited, the thing about stars is that, if they didn't actually exist, it would have been easy to prove that they didn't exist.

So, I believe that offering the worst possibility of all the possibilities of the universe is, at the very least, a responsible approach.

THE WORLD IN FIFTY YEARS

TRANSLATED BY ADAM LANPHIER

Written October 28, 2005, at Niangzi Pass
First published in *Global Entrepreneur*, 2005, no. 12

In a moment of carelessness, a time traveler left a flashlight in Song Dynasty China. A commoner found it and offered it up as a sacred treasure to the Imperial Household. Eventually, the batteries died, and the relic shone no more, leaving nothing but immense curiosity and confusion in its wake.

That's a story from a work of sci-fi. Arthur C. Clarke famously said, to paraphrase a bit, that to the people of a technologically primitive era, modern science would be indistinguishable from magic. As it turned out, he was a bit off the mark: The products of modern science have already surpassed the wonders of magic. First off, modern science deals with energy levels far higher than anything in the world of magic. Nothing in ancient mythology approaches the energy level of a twenty-megaton thermonuclear warhead. Sun Wukong's Golden Staff of Compliance, Zeus' thunderbolts—energy-wise, they're both a step down from the bomb. Secondly, mythology is concerned with a much smaller scale of space than modern science. The sphere of myth has a radius that seldom extends beyond the orbit of the moon, whereas humanity's space probes are on the verge of exiting the solar system.

Sci-fi writers imagine things differently from scientists and futurologists. They all envision large arrays of different futures, but scientists and futurologists ultimately choose to follow those visions they think most likely to happen, whereas sci-fi writers choose those they think have the greatest aesthetic potential as literature. Historically, sci-fi's been a bit overhyped as a predictive tool: The first submarine was built long before Verne wrote of one, and Clarke was just a nose ahead of science when he envisioned communications satellites. But in the interim, a dramatic fact became apparent: Scientists and futurologists were missing the mark, too. Scientists of the nineteenth century concluded that according to the principles of fluid dynamics, a train could go no faster than ninety miles per hour –any faster, and it would suck the air out of the cabins. At the beginning of the twentieth century, a sizable portion of physicists believed that humankind had achieved a comprehensive understanding of the laws of matter; we now know that there's an ocean of truth out there, and we're no more than children collecting shells on its shore, our shoes still dry. In the 1960s, one eminent scientist asserted that the world needed only a single giant computer. And look at *The Third Wave* and *Megatrends*, both published in the early eighties, both hailed as seminal works of futurology—and both almost entirely unrealized, in their macroscopic and specific predictions alike. This history of miscalculations has, in recent years, altered the course of futurological research, shifting its focus toward the analysis of near-term development policy. Its practitioners no longer presume they're able to forecast anything more than twenty years off.

It's an interesting thing, really: The rigorous, science-based predictions of scientists and futurologists and the spirited "flights of fancy" of sci-fi writers are just about equally (in)accurate! Reality stands as proof of this—neither method can predict what's going to happen, so why not just let our "fancies" fly?

The science-fictional imagination can leap ten quadrillion years through time to the death of the universe, but here, we'll just take a walk through the next half century or so, that being an era most readers of this essay will live to see. Remember: These are just imaginative guesses . . . but remember, too, that a rigorous, scientific prediction would have roughly the same odds of panning out.

ENERGY

Let's begin with one thing that's sure to happen in our imagined time frame: We *will* run out of oil, and despite its greater reserves, we'll run out of coal, too, sooner or later. The main alternatives to fossil fuel are solar, wind, hydro, tidal, and nuclear (both fission and fusion) power. The first four, though renewable, don't produce much power, which means they may not be scalable to the future's colossal appetite for energy. Therefore, the most promising contender for the alternative power source of the future is nuclear energy. Fission's already here and in use, but fusion, which promises a greater yield, has none of fission's problem with radioactive waste. Controlled-fusion technology isn't yet practical, but that day isn't far off—we're currently on the verge of a breakthrough. Halfway through our fifty years, the world will surely recognize its depleted fossil fuels as a crisis and invest vast sums toward fusion research, which will make controlled fusion a reality.

Fusion is an order of magnitude more productive than fission, and its feedstock is extracted from seawater, so there's no shortage there. Commercial fusion stands to make electricity a prodigious, dirt-cheap commodity, which will change human society in massive, profound ways, comparable to steam power's decline in favor of electricity and petroleum.

What will show up first is mobile energy transmission, also called wireless power, which transmits energy not through cables, but as microwaves from which consumers extract power. We could make this happen with current technology—in fact, we have, initially for a dubious purpose: wiretapping. Over the course of the Cold War, the US repeatedly zapped the Soviet embassy with microwave beams to recharge the bugs they'd installed inside. There are two reasons this technology isn't in wide use. The first is that it's inefficient—a significant portion of the emitted energy goes uncollected. But this won't be an issue once fusion is producing copious energy for next to nothing. The second is electromagnetic pollution. As yet, there's no way to fix this one, but that doesn't mean there won't be in the future. Remember—flight of fancy.

With mobile energy transmission, we'll be able to get electric power wherever and whenever we like, just as we can with cell signals today. This will upend our lives, most dramatically in the field of—

TRANSPORTATION

Once fossil fuels are tapped out, cars themselves will become fossils. Their disappearance, along with the advent of fusion power, will afford us a chance to correct a mistake we made at the start of the last century.

As soon as the airplane was invented and made viable, human society should have adopted flight as its main mode of transportation. 3-D space permits a speed and volume of traffic that's inconceivable on the 2-D ground. Even short-range, urban transport could be provided by versatile, low-speed flying cars—helicopters with blade-shields, say. The biggest barrier to the expansion of flight is its fuel consumption, as aircraft generally consume dozens of times more fuel than land-based vehicles. But two long-established bits of tech have the potential to reduce flight's fuel needs to a level comparable to that of land-based travel: airships and parasails. Airships are lighter than air and thus need no vertical propulsion, and parasails, though similar in principle to conventional aircraft, have large wings and little deadweight, which means they can generate a lot of lift without much force. Of course, both modes of aviation have substantial disadvantages—airships have a size problem, for instance, and parasails would need places to take off—but if we'd put all the R&D we've done in service of land-based travel into flying-car technology, I believe we could have solved these problems, and even invented more efficient means of personal flight. There's also the fact that you don't need roads in the air; flight would have saved us a fortune in road construction. In hindsight, the rapid development of land-based transportation was what killed air transport in the cradle; it made it impossible for personal aircraft to replace cars.

Fusion would render the energy consumption of personal aviation economically viable, and with mobile energy transmission, aircraft could harvest external power as they flew, so they'd need no heavy batteries. They'd be lightweight and maneuverable, and their range would be unlimited.

There might also be "sky trains" in the future: large, long-range aircraft with high-powered planes as their "engines," towing strings of unpowered gliders that serve as "carriages." There are no technological problems with the idea—in fact, in the Second World War, Allied forces captured an Axis-controlled bridge over the Seine using just such a "train," with a standard plane at its head and a trail of gliders that successfully deposited their loads of troops and equipment behind enemy lines. For a composite vehicle like this, takeoff and landing would be the tricky parts, so the sky train of the future could use mobile energy transmission to stay aloft indefinitely, and lightweight surface-to-air ferries could carry passengers back and forth.

In conjunction with this kind of large-scale conveyance, lightweight personal flight apparatuses will replace cars completely. Thanks to mobile power transmission, these devices, at their most compact, might be no bigger than an umbrella. Perhaps each commuter would fly to work with their own little umbrella-propeller.

Establishing this flying world of wonders would be possible only with sufficient fusion energy and mobile power-transmission tech. If there's been no breakthrough in fusion by the time we've exhausted our reserves of fossil fuels, and fission's limiting factors—fissile material supply, pollution, and so on—prove insurmountable, humanity may enter an age of energy scarcity. Of course, there's also the possibility that even after mastering fusion tech, humanity might preemptively impose energy restrictions, for environmental reasons and so forth, which would likewise bring about an age of energy scarcity. Travel by flight naturally couldn't go mainstream in such an era, so, once gas-powered cars are gone, how else might terrestrial travel appear?

It's nearly self-evident that we'd have cars powered by solar and other renewables, but that's no flight of fancy. Let's make our wild guesses wilder and step back into the age of animal-powered transport.

There's a romance to the pre-automobile era of horse-drawn carriages, and those vehicles had many substantial advantages over cars—advantages whose value would be even greater in the future yet to come. Manure is less of a pollutant and easier to manage than car exhaust; horses are incomparably more energy-efficient than cars; and the headache of feeding and tending to horses would subside as a by-product of animal transport's commercialization, which itself would become a huge, lucrative market.

Of course, the future era of the horse-drawn carriage will be no mere regression: The horse and carriage of the future will be kitted out with new technology. The most obvious drawback of the horse-drawn carriage, compared to the automobile, is its speed. This problem *can* be overcome. Here, the bicycle comes to mind: With the same physical effort one exerts traveling by foot, a bicycle triples or quadruples one's speed. It follows that it would be perfectly possible to design a bicycle for horses, adapted to that animal's four-hooved gait—with the right transmission and wheels, it would triple or quadruple a horse's speed, and the horse-drawn carriage would be comparable to the automobile, speed-wise.

The horse-bike would be a pure, low-tech piece of machinery, with four pedals and two gear chains for each horse. With a carriage, there might be four wheels; for a lone rider, two would suffice. In either instance, the conveyance would move at a satisfying clip on the highway, and with novel materials, it could be made light and flexible.

The horse itself will also be technologically modified. A genetically enhanced horse might be comparable in physical strength to the horse of yesteryear, yet no bigger than a large dog.

Let's send our thoughts farther still: What about horse-drawn carriages that *fly*? The aircraft that requires the least propulsion is the dirigible, as its buoyancy obviates the need for lift. Physically, a horse would be more than capable of powering a dirigible's propeller. As new materials emerge, creating a smaller, lighter, and faster horse-powered aircraft isn't outside the realm of possibility—human-powered aircraft are already a reality, after all. Let's follow this dream and see where it goes: Could we genetically modify some sort of large bird—an albatross, perhaps—such that humans could ride them? Or (last thought) could a horse's genes be modified to give it wings? Don't dismiss the idea outright. The people of ancient times could imagine riders in the sky, with birds and winged horses as their steeds, yet they never imagined anything like an automobile. If we can create things beyond our ancestors' imagination, why can't we make what they *did* imagine a reality?

Our fancy has now flown into another field whose future is full of wonders—

LIFE SCIENCES

The life sciences, with molecular biology leading the pack, are now on the verge of a breakthrough that will enable scientists to manipulate genetic material as if it were code and they were programmers. This technology promises miracles to rival the book of Genesis.

First, let's see where that thought takes us. Scientists could fabricate a biological engine, which would really be nothing more than a few strong muscles, wired with nerves. All the nutrition and energy it needed would be provided by an inanimate, mechanical system. For fuel, a living engine would consume organic "food"—some plant that can be grown in large quantities, say—which it would transform into energy with much, much greater efficiency than an old mechanical engine. If the horse and carriage isn't to your liking, just take a living car.

It will also become possible to synthesize food in factories. This technology will utterly alter the appearance of the world. Great tracts of farmland will be reclaimed by forest and grassland, and humanity will suddenly find itself with much habitable space. Centralized food synthesis will mark the beginning of humanity's true "return to nature."

But cultivators of the land won't disappear. There will still be people in the vast, new wilderness, dropping seeds here and there. Their crop will astonish us—they'll be planting *cities*.

With gene programming, we may be able to grow plants into whatever complex shape and size we may need. This technology is now in its infancy. At the beginning, we might make trees grow into the forms of various tools and furnishings; after that, we might have them grow into grand edifices, with a great variety of structures and interior layouts. When we get there, architects will double as gardeners. These house-trees would be habitable even when alive, and a forest of such trees would be nothing less than a city, a true *ecopolis*, at one with nature.

Many other impending technological breakthroughs in the life sciences will change our lives profoundly. One is the life-preserving tech of hibernation. If you happen not to like the era you're in, you can just hibernate into the future. Certainly, this tech will be prohibitively expensive at first—but it's also certain that a huge industry will form around it, which will lower the price to within the means of the average person. In the future's future, awakened hibernators will constitute a discrete social caste, which will no doubt cause problems for the people of those eras. Hibernation may dramatically change the structure of human society—short-term hibernation, for instance, may lead to grandfathers who are younger than their grandsons. And with a lot of hibernators, won't we need to consider future eras' ability to accommodate them? Such social issues are as troubling as they are fascinating.

The life sciences even have the potential to alter humanity's biomorphology—a form of self-determined evolution (or devolution). For example, a combination of human and fish genes might enable humankind to live undersea. This seems far-fetched at a glance, but just three years ago, scientists successfully grew a human ear on the body of a lab rat. So, post–food synthesis, humankind's habitable zone will expand once again.

Another, more significant change will occur when we locate the genes that control human height. As I have expressed in other writings, the idea of reducing the human body's height and volume—shrinking our own scale—would lead to an equivalent expansion of our living environment. If humans were shrunk to a third of their current height, we would consume far fewer resources, and to us, the Earth would be a much vaster world than before. On Earth today, the smallest mammals by volume that are reasonably similar to humans are rodents. With genetic engineering, humans could eventually shrink themselves to the size of house mice—perhaps without any loss to their brains' intellectual capacity. If each individual human shrunk themself to such a degree, the world would appear to them a fundamentally changed place. The Earth would be vast to them in a way that defies our imagination.

That humans will biologically alter themselves is inevitable, which makes life sciences the most terrifying of the sciences. They will shake humanity's definition of itself, and the boundaries between humans and other animals—even between human and plant—will begin to blur. It's hard to say what effects this may have on humanity's culture and spirit. The question of which people are *people* will come increasingly to haunt humankind. However, before this question turns deadly, it will be overshadowed by another issue that has to do with the way humankind lives. We turn now to this second issue. Genetic engineering has the potential to produce a host of other scary things—gene-seeking missiles, for instance. If someone wished to target and eliminate a person or group, all they'd need to know is their target's genetic makeup. With that, they could spread a highly contagious pathogen in their target's country, a germ whose infection causes mild, brief symptoms in ordinary people but is fatal to the target.

Here, our imagination has entered a field that, despite our reluctance to face it, demands a serious treatment—

WAR

We can be nearly certain of one more thing about the half century to come: War isn't going anywhere. Yet, strangely, as our fancy flies into the battlefield of the future, we find a measure of comfort there, in that place where rivers of blood once flowed. War itself is always barbaric, but war as it's waged could be a bit more humane. The use of nonlethal weapons is a hackneyed idea by now—in the future, a more humane style of warfare may emerge, one that avoids bloodshed and casualties altogether.

First, what we'd need is something to stand in for or simulate war. It would have to satisfy two criteria: It must represent with some accuracy the combined force of the belligerent nations, and second, the simulation must be run according to a protocol recognized by the belligerent nations and the international community, so that each side's will to fight and determination to win can influence the outcome to some extent. Think of the Olympic Games: A country's performance in an individual event—soccer, say—has little to do with its political, economic, or military might, but a country's aggregate performance across many Olympic events is a fairly accurate reflection of its overall power. Moreover, sports have the advantage of being among humanity's oldest pastimes, with established, universally recognized rules already in place. What's more, the Olympic Games have been and remain the world's largest and most consequential gathering. These factors would make the Olympics an ideal proxy for war. Of course, in the Olympic Wars, weak countries are bound to lose . . . but bear in mind that when traditional wars break out, weak countries are likewise doomed to defeat, and the awful price for that outcome is blood, paid by all the belligerents, especially the weak ones. Yet the Olympic Wars wouldn't just be a pretext for weak countries to surrender—each gold medal a defeated country has won in any individual event would earn them certain rights. For example, if a weak country's delegation were to lose to a strong country's by a single gold medal, they'd have lost the war, to be sure, but their relative medal count might change what that means considerably: Maybe they wouldn't be occupied, or their government would be kept in place and they'd be permitted to maintain a standing army, etc. All they'd have to do is destroy all their biochemical weapons and pay a third of the indemnities as listed in the ultimatum. The Olympic Wars will lead humanity, at long last, to renounce barbarism and become truly civilized. A country's prowess at sports will thenceforth be an important indicator of that country's strength, and in order to compete at the highest levels, countries will need broadly athletic citizenries to draw from; therefore, every country's enormous military expenditure will go instead toward improving its people's physical fitness, ushering in new, healthier, more civilized forms of community and international politics. And once war has lost its blood and death, it has the potential to undergo an inconceivable transformation—its value as a spectacle will come to the fore. The Olympic Wars will obviously be far and away more exciting and consequential than the Olympic Games, which also means big business. Establishing a system for the Olympic Wars will be the biggest political project humanity has ever undertaken. Accrediting the rules and outcomes of the competition, supervising the processes of the Wars, and other such work will be long and hard, but as human society advances, all these obstacles will become surmountable. If people are willing to die in war, why shouldn't they be willing to live at play?

If the "Olympic Wars" idea is a fever dream (. . . it sort of is), another low-casualty form of warfare—*digital occupation*—is much more likely to emerge. Digital occupation, as I'm calling it, refers to total control of an enemy country's information systems, without touching its sovereign land. In the future, internet-based information systems will be fundamental to a nation's survival. A country has two types of territory: its traditional, terrestrial territory and, superimposed on that, its digital territory. In the future, the latter may come to be more important to a country than the former—take control of it, and you'd effectively control the enemy's political and economic pulse. Furthermore, there are two sorts of digital occupation: the first is won through digital combat during wartime, and the second is imposed after a traditional war as a means for the winner to occupy its defeated enemy's territory. If a country thus occupied tried to free itself by destroying all its information systems, it would, in the fully digitized age to come, cause its economy to collapse and its government to lose control of the country.

The country would become a primitive power vacuum. A country's destruction of its own information systems would be no different from self-harm or suicide. So, in a plausible future, a strange, nightmarish scenario might occur: You wake up one morning, and everything is calm as usual—no smoke, no alarms, and not a single enemy soldier in sight. Cars are humming along the streets, parents and children are strolling in the park . . . but you've just been told: *You are a subjugated citizen of a conquered nation.*

Finally, we've come to computers and the internet. These things will do more than form the digital territory of nations; they will present human civilization in its entirety with a grave dilemma: the question of—

DIGITAL LIVING

The digitization of life will present humanity with an inflection in the arc of its fate more mythic than any it has faced before. Its arrival will herald either the end or the rebirth of human civilization. Before we get into that, let's imagine the next phase of the spread of computers and the internet.

At present, it's perfectly possible to make a computer mainframe as small as a cell phone or even a wristwatch. The problem is the display. There's a limit to how small traditional displays can get, and it has nothing to do with technology—if they're too small, you can't see them. To solve this problem, we may come out with a whole new species of display: retinal projection. The first step is to create a microprojector, comparable in size to the diameter of a hair. Given the advances we're making in nanomechanics, there's no technological barrier to our achieving this. Next, we'll need to mount this projector onto the lens of the eye and have it project images directly onto the retina. This will transform our eyes themselves into computer displays, with viewing areas so large and images so crisp that the eye would perceive them no differently than it does the real world, such that in the absence of other stimuli, it would be impossible for a person with a retinal projector to tell whether what they saw was real or a computer's projection. (By then, computers will be worn on the wrist, or as pendants, or as earrings.) Such a technology, in combination with our rapidly developing mobile communication tech, promises to incorporate computers and the internet into every person—another step toward an informatized, digitized world.

And retinal projection is just one of the breakthroughs we'll see in human-machine interface technology. Computers will come to understand natural language, and in addition to visual and auditory interfaces, there will be smell, taste, and touch-based interfaces, too—we may even see endocrine interfaces. People will thus be able to engage in as many ways with the virtual world of the internet as they do with the real world. Step by step, their sense-impressions of the virtual world will come to mimic their impressions of the real world, such that it will one day be possible to savor a gourmet meal or make love virtually.

Quantitative change eventually gives way to qualitative change. Once the majority of people are spending far more of their time in the online, virtual world than in the real one, human society will existentially shift from the real world to the internet, and the Life Digital will have come. Imagine it: their cities gradually falling silent, streets deserted; everyone in their room, eyes closed (to keep the sight of reality from interfering with their retinal projection), living their lives in the virtual world of the internet—the site of all their struggles and pleasures, for the rest of their lives.

We have no way as yet to evaluate the merits of such a novel mode of living, but before we try, we must not dismiss the idea as completely absurd. In the countless, crowded internet cafés that now dot our cities and countryside, this new mode of living has already begun to emerge. We can see, in the internet-engrossed teenagers that populate them, the dawn—or the shadow—of the era of digital living. Parents of that era will worry about their children's absorption in another world and set time limits on their engagement with it, and the issue will constitute a serious, widely discussed problem in society. What will be different is that the parents of the future won't be limiting their children's screen time, but their real-world time.

Digital living will radically reshape human society, with every one of its realms beyond recognition, including—

GOVERNMENT, ECONOMY, EDUCATION, CULTURE . . .

Once people and the internet have merged, national or even global referenda could be held at any time. This will profoundly change how nations and governments operate. If, as computing technology continues to advance, it makes such breakthroughs in processing speed and intelligence that web servers are able to rapidly process and synthesize all the information they receive, then the vast majority, or even all, of a country's citizens would be able to speak out and voice their opinions in unison, as if they were a single person. This would make it possible for a government to converse with all the residents of a city or a country, or even all the world's billions, simultaneously, as if talking with one person or small group.

Virtual products, things that exist only as numbers, will make up a significant portion of the economy. Even today, players of online games have already begun to trade virtual equipment. One could view this as the beginning of the virtual economy. In the future, every real-world commodity may have a digital counterpart online, each of which would have its own value.

The virtual world may also give rise to some unexpected, peculiar commodities.

There are three distinct stages of the digitization of life. The first is the stage of separation between human and machine, which has already begun. The second, as described above, is the integration of human and machine. The third is the pure digitization of life, in which it will be possible for a person to upload the entirety of their consciousness and memories onto the internet. The technology this third stage would require seems elusive at present, but once it's there, each person's memories and sensations might be available to others. A person's very life may become a commodity, and an epic, romantic life would be a thing of great value. Someone who's been to hell and back and lived to tell of it could certainly sell their life for an astronomical sum—*he who survives a disaster is due for a fortune,* indeed. In that era, manufacturing high-value lives is bound to become a career wherein people will do everything they can in the pursuit of adventure or romantic liaisons.

You might think of them as the successors of today's novelists, except their pen will be their life itself, whose difficulty and danger is hard to imagine. This industry may also become a corporate venture, with companies using every means and resource at their disposal to provide a segment of their workforce with the happiest possible lives—solely in order to produce a batch of happy lives to sell.

At a certain point in the development of human-machine interface technology, there will come to be network transparency in the connection between the brain and computers. Knowledge stored in a computer will be transferable to a connected person as a clear memory. What's more, we'll be able to plug a computer's algorithmic and information-processing capabilities directly into the brain, so that it serves as an amplifier of intellect and thinking. Human thought will rise to a higher plane. This, combined with the technology, described above, to upload neural information, may turn education into yet another thing beyond our ability to imagine: profundity of thought, perfection of psychology and character, refinement of artistic and aesthetic sensibility, and so on—they'll all become commodities, things to be bought and sold.

The biggest, least conceivable changes of all may be cultural. But of this one thing, we may be certain: Human culture is oriented toward ever-greater diversity. Even as our cultural iconography grows more consolidated, literature and art are becoming ever more decentralized, such that a "peer-to-peer" culture may eventually emerge—a culture in which a single person's creation may be meant for a single other to enjoy, or even one in which many people's creations exist to please just one person.

. . .

Here, our fancy seems to have flown into some wild, bold stuff, but these predictions are really nothing more than reasonable extrapolations based on existing technology. So long as technology continues to advance at its current pace, most of the things we've imagined here *will* come to pass.

But there exists another possibility that could suddenly turn the human world on its head. What would create favorable circumstances for this upheaval are—

BREAKTHROUGHS IN APPLIED FUNDAMENTAL PHYSICS

In its explorations of the most fundamental laws of matter, modern physics' achievements in the realm of theory have far outstripped its technological applicability in society. If some channel suddenly opened that connected the frontier of applied theory in physics to the domain of practical technology, it could grant humankind power great enough to alter the universe.

The cutting edge of theoretical physics—superstring theory—holds that matter, at its most fundamental scale, occupies eleven dimensions. As many as eight of those dimensions are strictly microcosmic. An important indicator of a civilization's technological advancement is the degree to which it can control and make use of microdimensionality.

Our first use of one of matter's microdimensions began when our naked, hairy ancestors first made fire in a cave, the control of chemical reactions being a one-microdimensional manipulation of elementary particles. Of course, our control of this dimension has advanced, from fire to steam engines, and from there on to electric generators. Humanity's one-dimensional control of elementary particles has now reached its zenith with computers . . . but all this is limited to control of a single microdimension. To a higher-order civilization out there in the universe, there's no essential difference between a bonfire and a computer—they both represent a single sort of control. This is the reason they'd see humanity, despite its progress, as a primitive species, or even as bugs.

Humans have begun to exert control over two- and three-microdimensionality in nuclear fission and fusion, in which particles are no longer single points, but things whose internal structures we can manipulate. But this is still a nascent sort of control, equivalent to our fire-in-a-cave stage of control over a single microdimension. At the forefront of physics, humans have exerted tentative four-dimensional control over elementary particles, though only within the confines of high-energy particle accelerators, which remain miles beyond any practical application. A major breakthrough in this regard is quite possible in the next half century, just as the atomic bomb came nearly out of nowhere in the first half of the twentieth century.

When humankind is able to control and exploit higher dimensions of matter, the power we'll gain is entirely beyond our capacity to imagine. Perhaps, as Arthur C. Clarke depicted, humans will be able to "[store] knowledge in the structure of space itself, and to preserve their thoughts for eternity in frozen lattices of light." At that point, man will be no different from God.

Here, our flight of fancy comes to its end. You're welcome to view these imaginings as a mere diversion, but to think they have nothing whatsoever to do with reality would be rash. Toward the end of the Qing Dynasty, people were already making use of electricity: The Empress Dowager Cixi lived to watch a movie, and the discovery of electromagnetic waves and their use in communications were just around the corner. But if a prophet of that era had predicted that within a hundred years, there would be a little gadget, just a hair bigger than a snuffbox, whose bearer could speak to anyone else holding one, even if that person was on the other side of the planet—people would certainly have thought that they were dreaming. Such an artifact could only have been a mythic, holy object, like the flashlight described at the beginning of this essay, left behind in the Song Dynasty. Yet now, there's one of these magic artifacts in each person's pocket.

HEARD IT IN
THE MORNING

TRANSLATED BY JESSE FIELD

Written September 26, 2001, at Niangzi Pass
First published in *Science Fiction World*, 2002, no. 1
Winner of the Galaxy Award for Readers' Choice Award

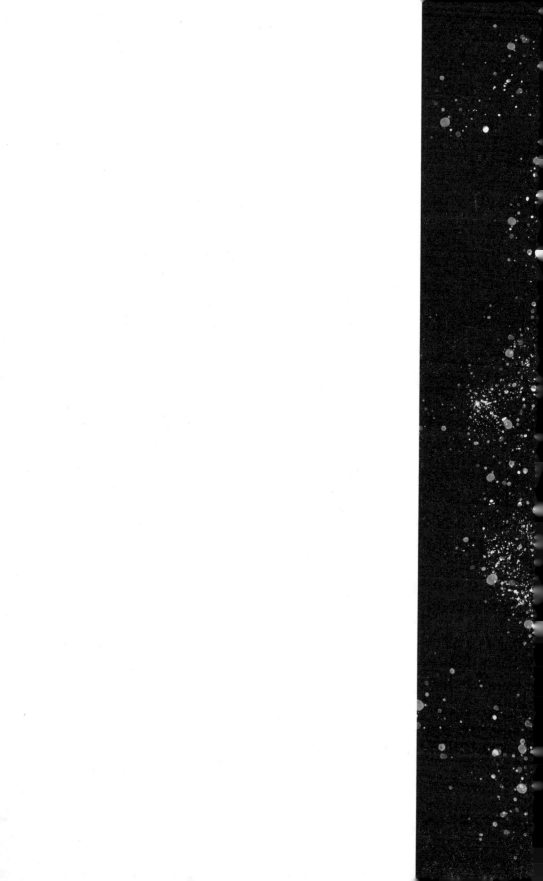

The Master said, "If I should hear the Way in the morning, I would feel all right to die in the evening."
—Confucius, *The Analects,* 4.8, translated by Annping Chin

EINSTEIN EQUATOR

"There's something I've been meaning to tell you," Ding Yi said to his wife and daughter. "Most of my mind is occupied with physics. I've only ever cleared away a small corner of it for you two. It's painful to admit, but there's nothing I can do about it."

"You've said that before," replied Fang Lin, Ding Yi's wife. "About two hundred times."

"Yeah!" added his ten-year-old daughter, Wenwen. "And I've said so, too, a hundred times."

"But you've never really understood, either of you," said Ding Yi, shaking his head. "You don't really get physics."

"That's fine," laughed Fang Lin. "I know it's not another woman. And that's all I care about."

The three of them were riding in a small vehicle traveling at five hundred kilometers per hour, along a steel tube five meters in diameter. The length of the tube was thirty thousand kilometers, encircling the entire planet at latitude 45° north.

The vehicle was entirely self-propelled, with a transparent carriage that had absolutely no apparatus for locomotion. When looking out from the vehicle, the steel tube projected forward, straight as a line. The vehicle within shot through like a bullet in a rifle barrel, albeit a rifle with no trigger or stock. The opening ahead seemed fixed at some infinitely distant point, unmoving, sharp as a needle. If not for the surrounding tube walls slipping by like gurgling water currents, there would hardly be any sense of movement at all. When the vehicle came to a stop, one could see that the tube walls were mounted with countless large instruments, as well as a great many hoops, all placed an equal distance apart. At full speed, the hoops became a blur, invisible to the naked eye. Ding Yi told his wife and daughter these hoops were used to produce a superconducting coil with a strong magnetic field, and the thin tube within the tube they could see suspended outside the window was a particle channel.

They were riding in the largest particle accelerator ever constructed by humanity, a device with a path around the planet, dubbed the "Einstein equator." With it, physicists could fulfill the fondest dream of the previous century's great scientists: a grand unified theory of the universe.

The vehicle was intended for use by engineers to service and repair the accelerator, but just now Ding Yi was using it to take his family on a trip around the world. He had long promised such a trip to his wife and daughter, though they never thought this was the route they'd take. The trip took sixty hours in total, and all they ever saw was the perfectly straight iron tube. But that was okay for Fang Lin and Wenwen, who were just happy to be together as a family for a couple of days.

And it's not like the trip was boring. Ding Yi would point at the tube walls from time to time and say to Wenwen, "Well, we are now passing Mongolia—can you see the grassy plains? Look, there are herds of sheep, too . . . Now we are going past Japan, though actually we're only just brushing against the northernmost tip of the country. Look, the sun is shining on snowy Kunashiri Island. You know, these are the first rays of light to fall on Asia each morning . . . And now we are way down at the bottom of the Pacific Ocean. It's so dark, we can't see anything. Or, wait, no, there are some rays of light here, dark reds. Ah, yes, we can clearly see, there is an ocean floor volcano. The magma exuding from it cools so fast, it's just dark red flashes that ignite and then extinguish again, like a big bonfire at the bottom of the ocean. Wenwen, here is where new continents are born!" And so on.

Later, they went past the entire United States in the vehicle, slipping past the Atlantic Ocean to the European mainland via France, driving past Italy and the Balkan peninsula, then entering Russia once again, and onward across the Caspian Sea back to Asia, passing into China via Kazakhstan. And now, they were on the last stage of the journey, returning to the Einstein equator's starting point in the Taklamakan

Desert, at the World Nuclear Center, which was also the main control center for the particle accelerator.

It was dark outside when Ding Yi and his family emerged from the control center building. The wide desert lay spread out beneath the stars, and all was quiet. The world was simple, yet so profound.

"All right, then," Ding Yi said to Fang Lin and Wenwen, excited now. "We three fundamental particles have now completed one accelerator experiment in the Einstein equator."

"Father, how long does it take for real particles to go around in the big tube like that?" Wenwen pointed at the accelerator tube behind them, stretching out from the control center east and west, away into the distance.

"Tomorrow, the accelerator will operate for the first time, with the largest particles it can handle, and each particle in it will receive a push like a nuclear weapon," Ding Yi answered his daughter. "They will accelerate to nearly the speed of light. At that speed each particle in the tube requires only a tenth of a second to travel the rotation course that just took us more than two days."

"Don't imagine that trip means you've kept your promise to us," Fang Lin teased. "That didn't count as a trip around the world!"

"That's right!" nodded Wenwen, playing along. "When you are free again, Papa, you have to take us along the outside of the tube, so we can see where we were when we were inside. Now that would be a real trip around the world!"

"Oh, there's no need for that," Ding Yi said to his daughter. He continued, with great feeling, "If you just use your imagination, this trip was enough. Why, you've seen everything already! From inside the tube, I mean. In your imagination. Remember: True beauty is not visible to the eye, but only to the imagination. It's not like the oceans or the flowers and forests; it has no color and form. You can grasp the universe as a whole, make the whole thing a toy for your own mind. But only with your imagination. And mathematics. Only then will you see this kind of beauty."

Ding Yi saw his wife and daughter off, but did not return home himself, instead heading back into the control center. Only a few staff remained on the overnight shift, marking it as one of the quietest times the site had seen after two years of construction and testing.

Ding Yi went up to the top floor and stood on the rooftop, open to the sky. As he looked at the accelerator tube bisecting the earth below, it seemed to him that all the stars were eyes and all the eyes were trained on the line below.

Ding Yi returned to his office below, lay down on the sofa, and went to sleep. It was then that a dream came to him, the kind only a physicist could have.

He was riding in a small vehicle, right at the starting point of the Einstein equator. It began to move, and he felt the massive power of the accelerator. He whipped along the forty-fifth parallel, one revolution after the other, like a ball on a roulette wheel. As he approached the speed of light, the dramatic increase in mass caused his body to feel like a solid hunk of metal. He grew conscious of the fact that his body contained the power to create worlds, and at once knew the pleasure of a god. On the last revolution, he was drawn down a side road and charged off to a strange place, where all was only void. He saw the color of the void: neither black nor white, but the color of colorlessness, though not transparent, either. Here, space and time themselves awaited creation. His creation.

In front of him, he saw a small black dot. It expanded dramatically, and he could make out that it was another vehicle, and inside there was another Ding Yi. Himself. They careened and collided at the speed of light, and disappeared, leaving only a dimensionless singularity in the midst of the void. This seed of all things exploded into a rapidly expanding high-energy ball of fire. Red light gradually faded, infusing into the universe, energy falling cold in the sky like snow. At first, a thin cloud of nebulae, and then fixed stars, star clusters, galaxies.

In this new universe, Ding Yi possessed a quantized self. He could leap from one end of the universe to the other in an instant. And not leap, even, but rather exist at all points in the universe simultaneously. He was like a boundless fog that permeated the cosmos. The silver desert of the fixed stars was igniting inside his body. He was everywhere even as he was nowhere. He knew his whole existence was an illusion of probability. His multi-centered spirit, churning in and out of existence, scanning the universe, seeking a vision of itself collapsing into a dense body. Even as he searched, this vision appeared. It came from two eyes which were floating in the cosmos, behind a silver curtain of star clusters. The eyes had the beauty and the long lashes of Fang Lin, but the lively spirit of Wenwen. These eyes scanned the boundless distance. But in the end, they could not perceive Ding Yi's quantized self. The wave function trembled, like a breeze over a placid lake, but it couldn't collapse into being. Just as Ding Yi was about to give up hope, the endless sea of stars did begin to coalesce. Nebulae began to swirl and surge. Then everything went quiet. The stars of the universe formed into a single large eye, an eye one billion light-years wide, its image like diamond dust scattered on velvet. It stared at Ding Yi. Then, in an instant, the wave function collapsed, like a film of fireworks played backward. Ding Yi's quantized existence cohered at last, at some tiny, insignificant point within the universe. He opened his eyes and returned to reality.

It was the control center's chief engineer who'd woken him. Ding Yi opened his eyes and saw the physicists and technicians of the nuclear center standing around him as he lay on the sofa. They looked at him like they had just seen a monster.

"What is it? Have I overslept?" Ding Yi looked out the window, and saw that the sky had brightened, though the sun had not yet risen.

"No," said the chief engineer. "But . . . something's happened." It was only then that Ding Yi realized that they weren't concerned with him, but something else entirely. The chief engineer dragged Ding Yi to the window. Ding Yi had only gone two paces when suddenly someone stopped him, held him fast. He turned. It was Matsuda Seiichi, the Japanese physicist and one of the previous year's Nobel Prize laureates.

"Dr. Ding," said Matsuda. "You may find your mind unprepared for what you are about to see. I . . . I wouldn't be too concerned about it. We might all be dreaming, at this very moment." Matsuda's face was pale; Ding Yi saw that the hand grasping him was trembling.

He could hardly suppress a shudder. "But I've just woken from a dream!" said Ding Yi. "What happened?" They all simply stared, agape. The chief engineer resumed dragging Ding Yi to the window. He looked out. What he saw made him immediately doubt the very words he'd spoken. The reality in front of his eyes was stranger than the dream he'd just had.

In the pale blue of the early morning light, the familiar accelerator tube bisecting the desert had been replaced with a band of green grass. Now a belt of green ran east and west, out to the horizon.

"Back to the control room!" called the chief engineer. Ding Yi followed them there and received yet another unbelievable shock: The control room was completely empty. Every piece of equipment had disappeared without a trace. Instead, all was grass, even growing directly out of the antistatic floor panels.

Ding Yi rushed madly out of the control room, around the building, and onto the band of grass, looking at how it disappeared off in the east, near the spot where the sun was about to rise. His breath came out in a fog in the cold desert air of the early morning.

"Where is the rest of the accelerator?" he asked the chief engineer, gasping.

"It has disappeared entirely—the parts aboveground, and underground, and in the ocean."

"And turned to grass?!"

"Uhm, no. The grass is only on the desert surface near us. In other parts, it has simply disappeared. The surface and the seabed parts are left with only empty abutments and the underground parts left with only an empty tunnel."

Ding Yi bent down and picked up a blade of the grass. Anywhere else, it would have been unremarkable, but here it was very unusual indeed: it looked nothing like the succulents or tamarisks of the desert, plants adapted to low-water conditions, but rather plum and crisp. Bursting with moisture, in fact. The kind of plant that could only grow in the south, with its higher rainfall. Ding Yi ground the blade of grass between his fingers, staining them green. A faint clean, grassy smell wafted toward his nose. Ding Yi stared for a long time into his hands. Then finally he said, "This does look like a dream."

But a voice from the east replied, "No, this is real!"

VACUUM DECAY

At the end of the green grass road, the sun was already half risen in the sky, its light shining straight in their eyes. Out of the rays of the sun came a person, moving toward them along the grassy road. At first it was only a silhouette backed by the sun, the edges swallowed up in the bright emerging wheel of light, making the figure seem like a mirage. But as it came closer, people saw he was an adult man. He wore a white shirt and black pants, but no tie. Closer still, his face also became clear: mixed Asian and European features, which was not unusual in this region, though no one would confuse this man for a local. There was something too regular about his features—they weren't quite realistic, more like an illustration of a human being on a public sign. When he came closer still, it became clear he was not of this world at all. Because he was not walking. No, his legs stood straight as pens, the bottoms of his shoes floating just above the grass. Then, just two or three meters from them, he stopped.

"Hello to you all. I have taken this external form so that we can communicate better. I do hope you can accept this, my best attempt at a human figure." The person spoke in English, and his voice was just like his face, extremely standard and without any distinguishing features.

"Who are you?" someone asked.

"I am the dehazardification officer of this universe."

This universe. Those two words left a deeper impression on the physicists than the rest.

"Did you have something to do with the disappearance of the accelerator?" asked the chief engineer.

"Yes. It was evaporated last night, as your planned experiment had to be stopped. By way of compensation I sent you this grass, which grows quickly in the desert."

"But . . . why?"

"Your accelerator, if actually operated to its maximum potential, can accelerate particles to power levels exceeding ten to the twentieth power gigaelectron volts, which approaches those of the big bang itself. And this could bring disaster to the universe."

"What disaster?"

"Vacuum decay."

Hearing this response, the chief engineer turned to look at the physicists by his side. They remained silent, their brows furrowed, as they thought it over.

"Do you need a more in-depth explanation?" asked the dehaz officer.

"No, there is no need," said Ding Yi, with a slight shake of his head. The physicists had thought the dehaz officer might bring up some concepts too difficult for humans to understand, but to their surprise, he referred to an idea proposed as early as the 1980s. At the time, most people thought it just a novel conjecture, with no relation to reality. Ideas like that had been all but forgotten by most.

The vacuum decay concept had made its earliest appearance in a 1980 article in the journal *Theoretical Physics*, by Sidney Coleman and Frank De Luccia, titled "Gravitational Effects of and on Vacuum Decay." Even earlier, Paul Dirac had theorized that what seemed to be vacuum in our universe could be a false vacuum, where in seemingly empty space, phantomlike virtual particles emerged and disappeared on unimaginably short time scales. In these instants, the living drama of creation and destruction went on endlessly at every point, making what we called a vacuum actually a teeming sea of particles. So it followed that a vacuum actually had an energy level. Coleman and De Luccia's contribution was to discover that certain high-energy processes might produce another vacuum state, one without the energy level of the present universal vacuum. The result might then be a "true vacuum" of energy level zero. Such a vacuum might only be the size of a single atom at first, but once produced, the higher-energy vacuum neighboring the lower-level vacuum would fall to the lower level, and so on, in a process whereby the low-energy vacuum volume would expand spherically and rapidly. The expansion rate of the sphere would quickly accelerate to the speed of light, and all protons and neutrons within the sphere's volume would instantly decay. All the matter in the world would evaporate, leading to total destruction.

"Within 0.03 seconds, the zero-energy vacuum sphere expanding at the speed of light would destroy the Earth. Five hours later it would destroy the solar system. Four years after that, it would destroy the closest star systems, and a hundred thousand years after that, the entire Milky Way galaxy . . . Nothing would be able to stop the expansion of the sphere, so in time nothing in the universe would escape." So said the dehaz officer, his words connecting precisely with what the physicists were thinking. Could he actually read their thoughts?! The dehaz officer spread his arms in a gesture of embrace.

"If we look at our universe as a wide sea, we are the fish in the sea. The boundless sea around us is so utterly transparent we forget it even exists. But I have to tell you: This is no seawater. It is liquid dynamite. A single spark could set off an inferno that destroys everything. As the universe's dehazardification officer, my job is to extinguish all potential sparks."

"I'm sure that's not easy," said Ding Yi. "Our universe already has a radius of twenty billion light-years, which must be a wide expanse even for a superior civilization like yours."

The dehaz officer smiled then—it was the first time he had smiled, and yet this smile, too, was entirely without distinguishing characteristics. "It's not as complex as you think. You already understand that our present universe is merely the embers of a big bang. Stars and galaxies are no more than scattered ashes that still retain some heat. You see, this is a low-base-energy universe, and the high-energy star systems you all see now only existed in the distant past. In the current natural universe, even the highest-energy processes, for example large masses cast into black holes, are all many orders of magnitude smaller than the big bang. In the present universe, the only chance for a big bang–level energy process comes from intelligent civilizations exploring with all their might the ultimate secrets of the universe. By concentrating great quantities of energy, they might create that level of power at microcosmic points. Hence, we only have to maintain surveillance over all the civilized worlds in the universe."

"But, how long have you been paying attention to humans?" asked Matsuda. "Perhaps since the age of Max Planck?"

The dehaz officer shook his head.

"So, was it the age of Newton? Also no? Surely not as far back as Aristotle?"

"All incorrect," replied the dehaz officer. "The universe's dehazardification systems operation agencies work like this: Many sensors have already been placed around the universe wherever life has appeared. When a civilization with the ability to produce big bang–level energy processes is discovered, the sensors issue a warning. A dehaz officer like myself receives the warning and then goes in person to observe the civilization on this world. But unless these civilizations are actually going to carry out experiments with energy levels on the order of the big bang, we absolutely do not interfere in any way."

Just then, a black square appeared above the dehaz officer's head, about two meters on each side. The surface of the square was of such a deep, bottomless blackness it looked like a hole dug out of reality. A few seconds later, the shadowy outline of a blue globe emerged from the black space. Pointing at this image, the dehaz officer said, "This is the image taken by the sensor placed at your planet."

"When was this sensor placed there?" someone asked.

"According to your geological division of time, during the Carboniferous period of the Paleozoic era."

"Paleo . . . what?!"

"But that was . . . three hundred million years ago!"

"Surely not as early as that?" said the chief engineer, his tone now one of awe and veneration.

"Early, you say? No, in fact, that was too late! When we first arrived at Earth during the Carboniferous period, we saw the Gondwana supercontinent, with its moist amphibious animals crawling in the primeval forests and swamps. Why, it all sent us into cold sweats of alarm! Clearly, Earth already long had the potential for a technological civilization, so the sensor should really have been in place from the Cambrian or Ordovician periods."

The image of the planet came forward, filling the square, the lens focused on the movements of the continents. Suddenly it felt like the scientists were carrying out the inspection themselves.

The dehaz officer said, "The image you are seeing was shot during the Pleistocene epoch, three hundred seventy thousand years ago, which to us is practically yesterday."

The surface on the image of the planet stopped moving, with the lens fixed on the continent of Africa, which was just then on the nightside of the planet, appearing as a large ink-dark patch surrounded by lighter ocean. Something had caught the sensor's attention: the image zoomed in, and Africa expanded into a more detailed view, quickly taking up all of the scene, as if the observer were on a nosedive toward the planet's surface. Darkness gave way to greater color contrasts: white at the accumulated snows of the fourth ice age and the darker parts remaining vague and unclear—whether they were forests or scattered rocks upon the plains, the audience could only guess. The lens continued to close in, until a snowy plain filled the scene, turning the display square entirely a single color, that of snow on the ground at night: grayish white, with a hint of dark blue. Then black spots on the snowy plain, quickly resolving into human figures. Next, one could see they were all hunched over, with long skins draped over their shoulders blowing in the wind. The image shifted once again, and the face of a person looked up to fill the screen. In the weak rays of evening light, there was no way to make out facial details, but they could see that humans had very high brows and cheekbones, and long, thin lips. The lens continued to zoom in, until it seemed it could go no further. A pair of deeply sunken eyes filled the screen, the pupils of the dark eyes filled with silvery dots of light at the center. These were the stars, reflected in the eyes.

The image froze on this frame and a sharp sound of alarm arose. This was the system warning, the dehaz officer informed them.

"Why?" asked the chief engineer, not understanding.

"When this early person looked up at the starry sky, the threshold for a warning was reached. For they have now expressed curiosity about the universe. And by then there have been ten of these supercondition events at different points, matching the conditions for a system warning."

"But if I'm not mistaken, you said just now that the sensor will only deliver its warning when a civilization capable of generating power levels equal to those at the creation of the universe emerges."

"Is not what you are looking at just such a civilization?"

The people looked at each other, all at a loss.

The dehaz officer smiled his traitorous smile. "Is it so hard to understand? Once life becomes conscious of the existence of the mysteries of the universe, it is only one step away from unlocking these mysteries." Seeing that the people still did not understand, he continued. "For example, life on this planet took four hundred million years to realize for the first time that the mysteries of the universe exist, but since then, only four hundred thousand years have passed, and you have constructed this Einstein equator. And the most accelerated phase of that development all happened in fewer than five hundred years. If you will, with their eyes on the universe in those moments, that human saw treasure. All of what you call human civilization since then has been little more than bending over to pick it up."

Ding Yi nodded his head as if he had begun to understand. "When you put it that way, the moment that person gazed up at the stars was monumentally important!"

The dehaz officer went on, "It is for that reason that I have come to your world, and set up surveillance over the progress of your civilization. It's as if I were looking over a child playing with fire, and the surrounding universe, illuminated by the fire, fascinates the child. But this child might lose control over the flames. And now, the universe stands in danger of being incinerated."

Ding Yi thought deeply on this. When he finally looked up, he asked what would become the most important question in the history of human science. "So what you are saying is, we can never obtain the grand unified theory? We will never plumb the ultimate mysteries of the universe?"

At this, all the scientists gazed questioningly at the dehaz officer, like souls awaiting their final judgment.

"There are many tragedies to a life of wisdom and this is one of them," the dehaz officer said blandly.

Matsuda, his voice quavering, asked, "As a higher civilization, how do you all accept such a terrible thing?"

"We are truly fortunate children in this universe, for we have obtained the unified theory."

Immediately, the fires of hope were reignited in the hearts of the scientists.

But Ding Yi thought of another terrifying possibility. "You mean . . . vacuum decay has actually happened, somewhere?"

The dehaz officer shook his head. "We used another method to obtain the unified model, which we cannot speak of now, though at a later time I may explain it to you in detail."

"And can we not repeat that method?"

The dehaz officer continued to shake his head. "Its time has passed, and no civilization in this universe may repeat it."

"Well, but, please, then tell us humans of the unified theory of the universe!"

The dehaz officer shook his head again.

"We beg of you! This is very important to us—no, it's everything to us!" Ding Yi rushed forward to grasp the dehaz officer by the arm, but his hands passed through the form of the man, feeling nothing at all.

"The Knowledge Protection Directive prohibits doing so."

"Knowledge Protection Directive?!"

"It is the highest directive regarding civilized worlds in the universe: A higher-level civilization is not permitted to transmit knowledge to a lower-level civilization. We call this behavior 'knowledge pipeline delivery.' Lower-level civilizations can only obtain knowledge by their own investigation."

"But that isn't rational!" cried Ding Yi in a petulant voice. "Better you all explained the unified theory to all of the civilizations seeking the deepest secrets of the universe, so they would not try to arrive at them via high-energy experiments. Wouldn't the universe be safer then?"

"Your thinking is too simplistic. The unified theory only covers this universe. As soon as you had it you would know that countless other universes exist, and then you would thirst for the trans-unified theory, to comprehend all of these universes. Plus, the grand unified theory would supply you with the knowledge to build technology that could generate even higher-energy processes, which you would use to try to tunnel through the barriers between different universes. But there are differences in the vacuum energies of different universes, so this would lead to vacuum decay, simultaneously destroying both universes, and maybe more. Knowledge pipeline delivery would also involve even more direct negative results and disasters in the lower civilization, for reasons that you all presently cannot understand. Therefore, the Knowledge Protection Directive must never be violated. What this directive refers to as 'knowledge' not only includes the deep secrets of the universe, but also refers to all of the knowledge you presently do not possess, including knowledge at each level. Imagine, for example, if human beings still did not know Newton's three laws or calculus—I would similarly not be able to give these to you."

The scientists fell silent. In their eyes, the sun which had just risen so high had sunk at once into darkness. To them, the whole universe in an instant became a grand tragedy, the depth of which they could not grasp immediately, but which would trickle over and through them for the rest of their lives. It would be torture. In fact, the rest of their lives would hold little meaning.

Matsuda sat down on the grass, dazed. What he said next would be famous later. "In a universe that cannot be known, my heart hardly cares to keep on beating."

These words expressed precisely what all the physicists were feeling, with their glazed and sluggish eyes. It looked as if they wanted to cry, but the tears wouldn't come. They were like that for some indeterminate time, until Ding Yi suddenly broke the silence.

"I've got it! I've thought of a way to get the grand unified theory without breaking the Knowledge Protection Directive."

The dehaz officer nodded at him. "Let's hear it."

"You tell me the ultimate secret of the universe. Then, you destroy me."

"I'll give you three days' time to consider this," the dehaz officer said, answering Ding Yi with neither surprise nor hesitation.

Ding Yi was wild with joy. "You mean this will work?!"

The dehaz officer nodded his head.

THE ALTAR OF TRUTH

What should people call the huge half-spherical body, its flat surface facing up and its round surface lodged in the desert, looking from far away like an overturned hill? The dehaz officer had constructed the half sphere out of sand, somehow causing a huge tornado to spring up out of the desert. In the midst of the wind, a tall pillar of sand had finally condensed into this form. No one knew what he had used to form so much sand into such a precise hemisphere shape, and of such strength and durability it could sit, lodged round side down, without collapsing.

But the hemisphere was unstable in this position, swaying visibly as gusts of wind passed over the desert.

The dehaz officer had told them that on his world this sort of hemisphere served as an altar. During the ancient age of that civilization, scholars had collected on such altars to discuss the secrets of the universe. Because of the instability of a hemisphere placed in this way, the scholars on the altar had to distribute themselves carefully over its surface, or else the hemisphere would tilt to one side, causing the people on it to slide off. The dehaz officer said little more about any deeper meaning the shape might have, but people guessed that it might symbolize the unbalanced and unstable state of the universe.

To one side of the hemisphere, there was a long sloping path, also made out of sand, that led from the ground up to the altar. In the dehaz officer's world, this path was not necessary, for even before they had become omnipotent, his race had been a transparent life-form equipped with two pairs of wings, and so they could fly directly onto the altar. The slope, then, was constructed especially for humans. Some three hundred of them would travel up the path to the altar of truth, where they would give their lives in exchange for the deepest secrets of the universe.

Three days before, after the dehaz officer had agreed to Ding Yi's request, new developments were driving the world to despair: in the space of a single short day, hundreds of people had made the same request. Besides the world's core scientists, other scholars from all over the world wanted it. At first it was only physicists, but later physicists and cosmologists, and then scientists from mathematics, biology, and all the basic sciences, and then even economists, historians, and others from outside the natural sciences. These people who asked to trade their lives for truth were all at the cutting edge of their fields, the elite even among the elite, with half of them winners of Nobel Prizes. The altar of truth had attracted the cream of the crop, as far as the human sciences were concerned.

The altar of truth was no longer in a desert, as the grass the dehaz officer had planted three days before had quickly spread, the band doubling in width, its unruly margins now just beneath the altar. More than ten thousand people had assembled on the grass: besides the scientists aiming to give up their lives and reporters from media organizations around the world, there were also the family and friends of the scientists. Two days and two nights of ceaseless pleading had left them all exhausted and sick at heart. But even with spirits at the edge of collapse, they still decided to give it their all, until the last minute. Helping them at this task were representatives from all the world's governments, including more than ten heads of state, all trying their hardest to hold on to the scientific elite of their countries.

"How could you bring our child here?!" Ding Yi demanded of Fang Lin, aghast. Behind them, Wenwen sat and played on the grassy ground, totally unaware of what was going on. She had the only happy face in a crowd of dark expressions.

"I want her to see you die," Fang Lin said coldly, her face pale and wan, her two eyes focused on the distance.

"Do you think her presence will stop me?"

"I don't hold out any hope for that, but I hope I can at least stop your daughter from being like you."

"You can punish me, but the child . . ."

"No one can punish you, and don't you pretend that what is about to happen is a punishment to you. You're finally making your dreams come true!" Lin yelled as she turned to face him.

Ding Yi looked straight into the eyes of his wife and said, "I guess you finally know me, on a deeper level."

"I don't know anyone. There's nothing in my heart now. Nothing except hatred."

"You of course have the right to hate me."

"I hate physics!"

"But if it weren't for physics, humans now would still be just animals living in forests or caves."

"Well, I'm hardly happier than them!"

"But I'm happy. I wish you could share in my happiness."

"Let your child share it with you, when she sees with her own eyes her father leaving her forever. At least then, after she's grown, she will stay away from physics. What poison it is!" Lin scoffed in disgust.

The heads of state were holding forth with the dehaz officer on the altar of truth, beseeching him to refuse the scientists' requests.

The president of the United States said, "Sir—if I may call you that? Our world's best scientists are all here. Surely you don't really want to destroy science on this planet?"

"It's not as severe as all that," said the dehaz officer. "Another batch of scientific elite will quickly surge forth and take their place, for exploring the secrets of the universe is the basic instinct of all intelligent life."

"Given we are all intelligent life-forms, how could you kill fellow scholars? Isn't that too cruel?"

"This is their own choice. Their lives are their own. And of course, can be exchanged for what they think is highest and most valuable."

"You needn't remind us of that!" exclaimed the Russian president. "We humans are long used to exchanging our lives for something higher. During the wars of the last century, more than twenty million in our countries did just that. But the fact now is that those scientists' lives get us nothing in return! Only they themselves will gain the knowledge they seek, and then you allow them only ten minutes more of life! They have become slaves to their desire for the final truth. Surely you too understand this to be the case?"

"What I understand to be the case is this: They are the only correct and reasonable living individuals in this star system."

The heads of state exchanged looks, then looked back in confusion and puzzlement at the dehaz officer.

The dehaz officer spread his arms as if to embrace the heavens: "Life is a small price to pay for the chance to glimpse the beauty of universal harmony."

"But after they see this beauty they only have ten minutes to live!"

"Even without the ten minutes, it would still be worth it to experience this ultimate beauty."

The heads of state looked at each other, all shaking their heads with wry and bitter smiles.

"With the progress of civilization, people like these will gradually increase in number," said the dehaz officer, pointing at the scientists gathered beneath the altar. "In the end, when the problems of existence are completely solved, when love disappears because individuation gives way to connection, and when art finally dies out upon reaching the final peaks of exquisiteness and obscurity, the pursuit of extreme beauty of the universe will become the only thing civilization can put its faith in. Then what these people want now will align with the basic values of the world."

The heads of state were silent a moment, trying to understand what the dehaz officer had said, when the president of the United States suddenly began to laugh. "Haha! Sir, you are having us on—you are playing a game with all of humanity!"

The dehaz officer looked confused. "I do not understand . . ."

"Humanity is not as stupid as you imagine," said the prime minister of Japan in reply. "Even a child could grasp fallacies in your logic!"

At this, the dehaz officer seemed even more confused. "I don't see any logical fallacies in what I've said."

The American president went on, after another wry laugh. "A trillion years from now, our universe will be filled with highly progressed civilizations. Well, if it is as you say, and the desire for the state of final truth will become the basic value of the entire universe, at that time all the civilizations of the universe will agree, use high-energy experiments to investigate the trans-unified theory that comprehends all of the universes—will they not worry that they will destroy everything, including themselves, in the course of these experiments? Do you wish to tell us that this will happen?!"

The dehaz officer stared at the heads of state for a long time without speaking, a strange gaze that made them shiver with its creepiness. One of them seemed to have a realization.

"Wait. You're saying . . ."

The dehaz officer raised a hand to stop him from going on, then walked toward the edge of the altar of truth. There, in a loud, bright voice, he said to all:

"You all certainly wish to know how we obtained the grand unified theory. Now this can be told to you.

"Long, long ago, our universe was much smaller than it is today, and very hot, too. The fixed stars had not appeared, but there were materials that had condensed from the energy, forming nebulae that permeated the red glow of space. Life appeared at this time—a kind of life formed from thin clouds of matter bound in force fields, with bodies that looked like tornadoes. This kind of nebulae life progressed rapidly as a flash, quickly producing an advanced civilization that spread all over the universe. When the nebulae civilization's own desire for the ultimate truths of the universe reached its peak, all the worlds of the whole universe agreed to risk the vacuum decay danger to advance experiments with big bang–level energies, in order to explore the grand unified theory of the universe.

"The nebulae life-forms' methods for controlling matter were entirely different from those of life in the universe today. Owing to the severe lack of matter in general, they made their own bodies into the things they wanted. After they made their final decision, some of the bodies on some of the worlds rapidly transformed themselves into accelerator parts. Finally, more than a million of these nebulae linked themselves up, forming a particle accelerator that could reach the energy levels at the creation of the universe. When the accelerator went into operation, a dazzling blue ring of light flashed among the dark red nebulae.

"They knew well the dangers of this experiment. As they recorded the results of the experiment, they transmitted the data through a gravity wave propelled outward, this being the only form that could carry information through a vacuum decay event.

"After the accelerator operated for a time, the vacuum decay event did occur. The lower-energy vacuum sphere expanded from atomic size at the speed of light, expanding in the blink of an eye to astronomical size, evaporating and utterly destroying everything inside. Eventually, the speed of vacuum sphere expansion exceeded the expansion of the universe itself, and after enough time had passed, the entire universe was destroyed.

"A long time passed, and the universe had nothing in it at all. Then, the material which had been evaporated slowly began to re-condense. Nebulae appeared again, but the universe was entirely dead and alone. Until, that is, the fixed stars and planets appeared, when life finally once again sprouted in the universe. In those early days, the gravity wave sent forth by the extinct nebulae civilization continued to reverberate, though the appearance of solid matter caused it to swiftly diminish. But just before it was entirely lost, the earliest civilization to appear in the universe intercepted it, and the information it carried was decoded, so that from this ancient experimental data the new civilization obtained the grand unified theory. They discovered that the most crucial data for building the model was produced in the last one ten-thousandth of a second before the vacuum decay.

"Let us consider the situation of the nebulae universe. Even as the vacuum sphere expanded and destroyed the universe, the worlds outside the sphere, beyond the sphere's event horizon as they were, could not have seen the catastrophe coming. So up until the moment the vacuum arrived, these worlds were entirely focused on receiving data from their accelerator. One ten-thousandth of a second after they had enough data to build the grand unified model, the vacuum sphere destroyed everything. However, the speed of thought among the nebulae was so high, one ten-thousandth of a second was a relatively long time for them. Therefore, they could have deduced the grand unified model in their last moment of life. Of course, this could be mere self-consolation. More likely, they did not deduce anything. Which means the nebulae civilization ripped open the fabric of the universe, but they themselves were destroyed before glimpsing the ultimate beauty of the universe. Perhaps they deserve our respect all the more, when we realize they knew the risks even before they began their experiments, and sacrificed themselves even as they supplied the data on the ultimate secrets of the universe to distant future civilizations.

"Now you all should understand that the pursuit of the most ultimate truth of the universe is the final aim of civilization."

The dehaz officer's story made everyone enter a long period of silent thought. Whether the humans of Earth agreed with his last sentence or not, one thing was sure: He had just left a permanent impression on human thought and culture.

The American president broke the silence. "You have painted a dark vision for civilization! Is it really true that in the long course of time, all humanity's hope and hard work just comes down to the moth flying into the flame?"

"The moth certainly does not find it dark. To the moth, there is at least a brief period of light."

"Humanity absolutely cannot accept such a view of life!"

"This is entirely understandable. In our universe reborn after vacuum decay, civilization is still in its early stages, and every world has its own ways, pursuing different aims. To the majority of worlds, the pursuit of ultimate truth does not possess the highest meaning. To risk the danger of destroying the universe for it would not be fair to the majority of lives in the universe. Even on my own world, certainly not all members agree to sacrifice all. Therefore, we ourselves have not continued trans-unified model high-energy experiments, and have set up the dehazardification system throughout the entire universe. But we believe that with the advance of civilization, there will finally come a day when all of the worlds of the universe will agree on the ultimate aim of civilization. Even right now in your infant civilization, there are already people who agree with this view.

"All right, the time has come. If any of you do not wish to exchange your life for truth, then please go back down and allow those who do so to come up."

The heads of state went down from the altar of truth and, when face-to-face with those scientists, made their last effort.

The president of France said, "How about this: Let us put the matter off a bit! Come with me! There is more to life for us to experience. Let's relax. Listen to the songs of the birds at dusk. We'll stare at the silver moon, as old familiar music plays. We'll drink our wine, and think of those we love . . . Yes, yes, you will discover that the ultimate truth is not so important as you first thought. There is more beauty in life than in the harmony of the universe!"

"All life follows reason," replied a physicist, coldly. "You will never understand."

The French president wanted to say more, but the president of the United States lost patience. "Fine! It's no good playing fiddle for the cows! Can you not see what a group of irresponsible people this is? What a bunch of con artists and deceivers they are?! They all whooped it up about doing research for the benefit of all mankind, when actually they just take society's wealth to satisfy their own perverted desires for some kind of mysterious beauty. Is there really any difference between that and using public money to visit a prostitute?"

Ding Yi rushed up and patted the president on the shoulder, saying with a laugh, "Well, Mr. President, science has come all this way and now, at least, someone can better define its fundamental character and substance."

Matsuda, off to one side, said, "We have long admitted his point and told you so; it's just that you never believed us."

THE EXCHANGE

The exchange of life for truth began.

The first group of eight mathematicians came up the long sloping path to the altar of truth. There was no wind over the desert sands, as if nature itself held its breath. All was silent. The just-risen sun threw long shadows from the humans onto the desert, and these shadows were all that moved in a world now frozen.

The figures of the mathematicians disappeared onto the altar of truth, invisible now to the people below. All kept still, listening with bated breath. Then came the voice of the dehaz officer, crystal clear in the tomb-like silence:

"Please ask your question."

Then the voice of a mathematician said, "We wish to know the final proofs of the conjectures of Fermat and Goldbach."

"All right. But the proof is very long, and there is only time for you to see the key portions. The rest can be explained in writing."

Just how the dehaz officer conveyed the knowledge to the scientists would forever remain a mystery to humanity. In images from a distant surveillance plane, the scientists all turn their heads up at the sky, though there didn't seem to be anything in the direction they looked. It was commonly held that the aliens had used some kind of thought waves to directly input the information into their brains. But in fact, the actual situation was considerably simpler: The dehaz officer projected the information into space. To the people on the altar of truth, the entire sky had become a display screen, but the information was not visible from any other angle.

An hour passed before someone broke the silence on the altar of truth. "We are finished," they said.

"You all have ten minutes," came the placid, if solemn, answer of the dehaz officer.

The altar of truth filled with the surreptitious sounds of many people deep in conversation. The people below could only make out fragments of what was being said, though their excitement and joy was all too evident. They sounded like a group of people who had been traversing dark tunnels for a year or more, suddenly coming to the light at the mouth of a cave.

". . . This is totally new . . ."

". . . How could it be . . ."

". . . before we intuited that . . ."

"Good god, it's really . . ."

When the ten minutes were about to conclude, another clear voice sounded on the altar of truth: "Please accept the sincerest thanks from the eight of us."

A strong light flashed on the altar of truth. When it was over, the people below saw eight orbs of ionic flame rise up from the altar, floating lightly upward, fluttering as they rose, gradually fading, bright yellow turning soft orange, and then red. Finally, they disappeared one by one into the blue sky. The whole process went on in complete silence. From the surveillance plane, one could see that only the dehaz officer remained on the altar of truth, standing in the center.

"The next group may ascend!" he called out in a loud voice.

As nearly ten thousand people fixed their eyes on the scene, another eleven people walked up to the altar of truth.

"Please ask your question."

"We are paleontologists. We want to know the real reason the dinosaurs were destroyed."

The paleontologists also looked up at the sky. They took much less time than the mathematicians who had been there before, and soon after someone said to the dehaz officer, "Now we know! Thank you."

"You all have ten minutes."

"Well, the puzzle pieces all fit . . ."

"I wouldn't have thought of that in my wildest dreams . . ."

". . . did you ever see anything so . . ."

And then the strong light appeared and disappeared. Eleven flaming orbs rose from the altar of truth, and were quickly lost in the skies over the desert.

Group after group of scientists walked onto the altar of truth, completed the exchange of life for truth, and then with a flash of a bright light were transformed into beautiful flaming orbs that floated away.

All was conducted in quiet austerity. Under the altar of truth, people avoided creating scenes of wailing for loved ones never again to be seen. Rather, the people of the world quietly watched the majestic scene, their own souls deeply cowed as some of their fellow humans experienced the greatest spiritual baptism in history.

A full day passed without anyone seeming to notice. The sun had fallen halfway toward the horizon in the west, the dusk scattering on the altar of truth with a layer of golden, shimmering light. The physicists began their ascent to the altar. These formed the biggest group, with eighty-six people. Just when they began, the voice of a child broke the silence that had held until that moment.

"Papa!" Wenwen, in tears, rushed out from among the crowd on the grass, ran straight to the sloping path, and charged into the group of physicists, clutching Ding Yi by his leg. "Papa, I won't let you turn into one of those balls of fire that floats away!"

Ding Yi lightly embraced his daughter. "Wenwen," he asked. "Tell Papa, can you remember the worst thing that ever happened to you?"

Wenwen, sniffing back her tears, thought for several seconds, then said, "I've been growing up out here in the desert, and I . . . I wanted so bad to go to the zoo. Last time, Papa went south for a meeting. You brought me to a big zoo, but as soon as we went in, your phone rang, and you said something urgent happened at work. The zoo only allowed children with adults, so I had to leave with you. You never took me there again. Papa, this was the worst thing that happened to me. I cried on the plane the whole way back."

Ding Yi said, "But, my child! You will certainly have a chance to visit that zoo again. Mama can take you. With Papa now, it's different. He's also at the entrance to the big zoo, and inside are the mysterious things Papa always dreamed of seeing. But if Papa does not go now, later there will never be another chance."

Wenwen stared at her father with her tear-filled eyes a moment, nodded her head and said, "Then . . . then go, Papa."

Fang Lin came up, took her daughter from Ding Yi's arms, eyes glaring at the altar of truth that loomed before her, and said, "Wenwen, your father may be the most selfish papa in the world . . . but he really does want to go to that zoo."

Ding Yi's eyes were fixed on the ground as he spoke again, his voice soft as a prayer. "Yes, Wenwen, Papa really wants to go."

Fang Lin fixed her baleful stare at Ding Yi one last time. "You are a fundamental particle all right—utterly cold. Go on, then. Off to your final experiment."

The group was about to turn and go when another female voice made them stop again.

"Matsuda-san, if you are going up there, I'll die right here in front of you!"

The woman speaking was a petite young Japanese woman, standing on the grass by the edge of the platform slope, a small silver handgun held against her temple.

Matsuda walked out from the group of physicists and up to the young woman. "Motoko," he said, looking her straight in the eye, "do you remember that cold morning in Sapporo? You said you wanted to test whether I truly loved you or not. You asked me, if your face were disfigured in a fire, what would I do? I said I would stay loyally by your side for the rest of your life. But you were disappointed when you heard this. You said that if I truly loved you, I would say I would blind myself, so that a beautiful Motoko would always exist in my heart."

The gun Motoko held did not move, but her dark eyes filled up with tears.

Matsuda Seiichi went on, "So, my darling, you know deeply the importance of beauty to a human life. And now, the ultimate beauty of the universe is before me. I must see her."

"If you take another step I'll shoot!"

Matsuda Seiichi smiled at her, then said softly, "Goodbye, Motoko." Then he turned and joined the other physicists as they started up again. Neither the sharp report of the gun, nor the splatter of brain material onto the grass, nor the soft thud of the body hitting the ground could make Matsuda turn around again.

The physicists reached the round surface of the altar of truth. In the center, the dehaz officer smiled warmly in greeting. The last light of the dusk went out as the sun set below the western horizon. Desert and grass alike went dim. The altar of truth seemed to suspend over the infinite black depths of space, reminding all of the physicists of the dark night before the creation of the universe, before a single star existed. The dehaz officer waved his hand. The physicists saw a golden star appear, in the distant black depths. At first it was too small to make out, but gradually it grew from a bright point to something with surface area and shape. They saw that it was a spiral galaxy floating toward them. The galaxy grew rapidly, displaying its roiling gases and nebulae. As the distance closed in still more, they discovered the stars in this galaxy were all numbers and symbols, the waves and structures forming one full, organized equation.

The grand unified theory of the universe had begun its slow and majestic passage before the physicists.

When the eighty-six orbs rose from the altar of truth, Fang Lin's eyes fell to the grassy ground. But she heard her daughter ask in a faint voice, "Mama, which one is Papa?"

The final person to ascend was Stephen Hawking, his electric wheelchair moving slowly up the long slope like a bug crawling up the branch of a tree.

At last, the wheelchair reached the altar and the dehaz officer at its center. By then, the sun had already gone down, and the indigo sky was scattered with stars, the desert and grass below too dim to make out.

"Your question, Dr. Hawking?" asked the dehaz officer, expressing no more respect for him than for any other, but facing him with his featureless smile as he listened to the impersonal inflections of the voice on the scientist's wheelchair loudspeaker.

"What is the purpose of the universe?"

No answer appeared from the sky. The smile disappeared from the dehaz officer's face, and some slight expression—despair?—seemed to flash across his eyes.

"Sir?" asked Hawking.

Silence. The sky still was a dark expanse. Behind some thin wisps of cloud, the star systems of the universe continued to churn.

"Excuse me? Sir?" asked Hawking, again.

"Professor Hawking, the exit is to your rear," said the dehaz officer.

"This is your answer?"

The dehaz officer shook his head. "I'm saying that you can go back where you came from."

"You do not know?"

The dehaz officer nodded. "I do not." Just then, he appeared not only human, but an individual with a full personality, as a dark flush of sorrow came into his face. Seeing him then, one could not doubt that he was indeed a person. And all too human, perhaps.

"How could I know," murmured the dehaz officer.

EPILOGUE

One night, fifteen years later, on the grassy plain that had once been the Taklamakan Desert, a mother and daughter were having a conversation. The mother was in her forties, but white hair had long appeared at her temples, her weather-beaten eyes filled with worry, exhaustion, and little else. The daughter was a slim and delicate young woman, her large and limpid pupils glittering with the reflection of starlight.

The mother sat upon the soft lush grass, her eyes looking dispiritedly at the distant horizon. "Wenwen, first you were admitted to the physics department at your father's alma mater, and now you are about to undertake doctoral studies in quantum gravity. And I've never tried to stop you. You can become a theoretician, and you can put all your spirit into this one field, if you like, but Wenwen, listen to your mother. Please, dear, no more than that. Don't cross the line!"

Wenwen looked up at the glittering Milky Way, saying, "Mama, can you imagine, all this came from a small point, twenty billion years ago? The universe crossed its line long ago."

Fang Lin stood, grabbed her daughter by the shoulders, said, "Child, please don't be like that!"

Wenwen's eyes were still fixed on the stars, unmoving.

"Wenwen, are you listening to Mama? What's the matter with you?!" Fang Lin shook her daughter, but Wenwen's eyes were still absorbed by the sea of stars.

Instead of answering, she asked her mother, "Mama, what is the purpose of the universe?"

"Ah . . . Noooo." Fang Lin gave up. She fell back to the grassy ground, her hands over her teary face. "Child, no, no, not this."

Wenwen finally turned her gaze back, squatted down, and held her mother by the shoulders, saying softly to her, "Then, Mama, what is the purpose of humanity?"

Like a block of ice, the question chilled Fang Lin's burning heart. She turned to look her daughter in the eye. Then she looked out into the distance, in thought. Just as fifteen years earlier she had looked in that direction. Where the altar of truth had loomed, and beyond, where the Einstein equator had once crossed the desert.

A light breeze sprang up, rippling the soft grassy sea, as if it were the sea of humans roiling beneath the infinitude of the stars, singing quietly to the universe.

"I don't know. How could I know," murmured Fang Lin.

ON *BALL LIGHTNING*

An Interview with Liu Cixin

TRANSLATED BY ADAM LANPHIER

Interviewed on May 23, 2004

First published in *Nebula II * Ball Lightning* in July 2004 by Sichuan Science and Technology Press

Reporter: We're delighted you've agreed to this interview. You've won the Galaxy Award five times now, and I'm sure after reading *Ball Lightning*, many readers will want to know more about the "hen that laid the eggs," so to speak. Could you tell us a bit about your process in writing *Ball Lightning*?

Liu: I salvaged the concept for *Ball Lightning* from another novel I abandoned, which depicted a near-future war. My short story "Full-Spectrum Barrage Jamming" took material from that same novel, so that story is vaguely linked to *Ball Lightning* in terms of characters and plot. But in spirit and essence, they are different works: The pure idealism and hero worship of "Full-Spectrum Barrage Jamming" is mostly gone in *Ball Lightning*, and something more complicated and strange stands in its place. There wasn't much war stuff that made it into the novel, either; what's left is relegated to the distant background.

The novel took four years to get published, but the actual writing process didn't take long—about a season, all told. The manuscript spent most of its time with the publisher. A friend of mine wrote a review of the manuscript online, which led some readers to the mistaken belief that the novel had already been published. That wasn't the case; the current publication is the novel's first time to print, and it's entirely different from the early draft my friend reviewed.

Reporter: What's your verdict on the novel? Do you, as the author, feel this novel is somehow different from your earlier works? What do you believe is critical in long-form works of sci-fi?

Liu: *Ball Lightning* is a relatively "pure" work of sci-fi. It's one of the most technical stories I've ever written. Depictions of technology actually overwhelmed the first draft a bit, so a lot of that content was cut in the second draft.

Still, I feel that the biggest difference between *Ball Lightning* and my earlier works is that it's packed with details. It's not a large framework built of grand scenes. As I wrote in an essay not long ago, "Along with its macro-details, it has a wealth of micro-details."

I think the most important thing in long-form sci-fi is creating a sci-fi *figure*. This means a nonhuman figure, or at least not a "human" figure as the mainstream literary tradition would have it. In a long-form work that's set far from reality, this figure might be a whole world of the imagination; in works that are negligibly far from the real world, it might be an imagined, as-yet-unknown object. *Ball Lightning* belongs to the latter category. It's a conscious attempt to manifest my concept of sci-fi, to create a nonhuman yet vivid sci-fi figure, which is something only science fiction literature is capable of creating.

Reporter: You mention at the beginning of the novel that the description of ball lightning in the work is based in rigorous scientific records of the phenomenon. Are you worried that experts on the subject or sci-fi fans will criticize the technical details?

Liu: Ball lightning is a complicated mystery of nature. As yet, there's no theory to explain it and no understanding of its causes. Its internal temperature is superhot—tens of thousands of degrees—but its surface is cool. What's most amazing about it is the selectivity of its energy release. There's a historical abundance of eyewitness accounts of incredible events that also appear in the novel, such as ball lightning incinerating people but leaving their clothing entirely unscathed. Not long ago, Russian scientists claimed to have generated it in the lab, but soon learned that what they'd made was a droplet of liquid with an electrically charged surface, which is not the same thing as ball lightning as it appears in nature. As stated in the preface, the ball lightning in the novel is just a sci-fi literary figure, a rendition of a sci-fi aesthetic; it shouldn't be taken as a scientific explanation of the phenomenon. In truth, my own (naïve and amateurish) scientific speculations about ball lightning are quite different. The novel's explanation isn't intended to be as logical as possible; it's meant to be intriguing and romantic.

As to criticism of technical details, I'll repeat what a master of sci-fi once said: If you're looking for technical errors, you've come to the right place.

Reporter: In your afterword, you make repeated reference to a number of wonderful worlds created by sci-fi greats and expressed your fondness for self-consistent, imaginary worlds. Does *Ball Lightning* live up to this criterion of yours?

Liu: If you look at sci-fi stories (full-length novels, especially) in terms of their adherence to reality, you'll find that most fall into one of two categories: They either build their own, complete worlds of the imagination, Creator-style, that are more or less unrelated to the real world, or they set off sparks of sci-fi in the real world—they toss diamonds into the grit of the real world, against whose grayness they sparkle all the more brilliantly. Works like the Foundation series and *Dune* belong to the former category, while works like the recently published *Darwin's Radio* belong to the latter. *Ball Lightning* is likewise an amalgamation of sci-fi and reality. As the postscript says: The world of the novel is the gray world of reality, the gray sky and clouds we know, gray mountains and waters and seas, gray people with gray lives—yet a little, transcendental thing floats atop this gray reality, like a star in a dream whose light laps across the boundary of the real, hinting at the majesty and mystery of the universe . . .

Reporter: I've found the scientists in your work to be different from how people generally picture them. They have a special sort of "madness," and the "madder" they are, the more brilliant. Take *Ball Lightning*—the protagonist almost loses his status as such a number of times and is nearly replaced mid-book by Ding Yi, a maverick physicist with a supporting role before he comes to the fore. Do you see this as an accurate portrayal of scientists, or is it more of a metaphysical or philosophical statement?

Liu: Professional researchers are a common thing nowadays, and naturally, most of them are normal people, but there are and always have been eccentric geniuses in their midst. Mainstream literature doesn't place much value on such figures because they're not tropes of the milieu that's typical of such literature. But the typical milieu of sci-fi is quite different from that of mainstream work, and it permits such figures to exist. Uncommon people crop up more often in sci-fi than in mainstream literature, almost by definition. To speak about *Ball Lightning*'s Ding Yi in particular, he's not at all the same as the character in "Heard It in the Morning"—he's got a number of real-world blemishes. And in point of fact, the book's protagonist *is* a normal person.

Reporter: You've frequently been criticized for the lack of "real people" in your work. Critics have said your characters are like ciphers—the women, especially. Lin Yun, the female lead in *Ball Lightning*, is a big departure from this.

Liu: Actually, the female lead of *Ball Lightning* is characterized simply, too. The reason you think she's different from my previous characters is that she's a different kind of person. She's no hero, and she's not an idealist; in fact, she's arguably not even a good person. Her childhood and circumstances while growing up made her thinking as cold as a machine's, and a bit warped, too . . . But as I said, the literary figure that *Ball Lightning* endeavors to create isn't a heroine—it's ball lightning.

I'd like to digress a bit here and say that some people may question the way the female lead behaves or the role she plays in the novel. As the author, I, too, sincerely wish that her characterization were implausible. Unfortunately, it isn't—reality is much, much more complicated than the postulates and laws of theory.

Reporter: Many of your works feature a substantial sense of realism and an exuberant patriotic fervor—"Fire in the Earth" and "Full-Spectrum Barrage Jamming," for instance—and *Ball Lightning* is no exception.

How do you view this strain in your work? Isn't it a bit odd to maintain a national standpoint in sci-fi literature, which promotes a panhuman perspective?

Liu: You may be thinking by inertia here. *Ball Lightning* might have the "substantial sense of realism" you mention, but there's really no "exuberant patriotic fervor" in it, nor is there any nationalistic stuff at all—and there's definitely no element of wish fulfillment. China doesn't win the book's war in any meaningful way; like the rest of the world, it's left trembling at macro-fusion, which is a more fearsome threat than war. Yet the detailed descriptions in the novel are realistic, too, particularly implications about the current state of the military in the character of the female lead. Still, as I said above, this is meant only to add to the novel's sense of immediacy.

As for my previous works, their sense of realism and patriotism varies based on their subject matter. There's no sense of realism in "Cloud of Poems" or "The Micro-Era," and there's no patriotism in "Devourer" or "Heard It in the Morning." As you said, science fiction is indeed the literature of panhumanism—but that doesn't seem at odds with it having a national standpoint. Would you expect a wartime traitor from 1940 to sacrifice their life for the civilizations of Earth in 2140?

Reporter: You've made remarks in the past about "stripping sci-fi from literature" and "macro-details," which indicate that there are big differences between your views on the genre and the views of its readers, even those of fans. If the market and readership were removed from the equation, what kind of sci-fi would you write?

Liu: What I want to write most is the kind of sci-fi that gives free rein to my imagination, that lets my thoughts wander without cease between the macro-est macro and the micro-est micro. I'm talking specifically about stories like "Sea of Dreams" and "Cloud of Poems." Frankly, those are the two stories I'm fondest of. Writing that kind of sci-fi is a pleasure, a "billion-year spree." (That's the title of a book on sci-fi theory by Brian Aldiss.)

Unfortunately, readers don't approve of works like these. I respect their wishes and won't write any more works in that series. But ideas like those are constantly popping up in my head, and they bring me endless pleasure. It's become a fascinating mental adventure for me. I still feel that's what fantasy literature, including sci-fi, is for.

Reporter: Last question: What do you see in store for mid- and long-form sci-fi in China? Have you hatched any new creative plans in the last few years that will keep you as the bellwether of the science fiction market?

Liu: I'm just an engineer and sci-fi writer, and I'm out in the middle of nowhere. I'm really unqualified to talk about the market. In the US, the era of sci-fi in magazines gave way to an era of full-length novels. I wonder whether Chinese sci-fi will follow the same path. My sense is that we'll need one or two novels that sell a million copies before the market for long-form works takes off, plus film adaptations of them that take in a hundred million yuan, or hit TV adaptations that CCTV airs during prime time. So far, at least, there have been no signs of either of these "holy grails."

My creative plans . . . we amateur authors aren't completely free to make decisions about that stuff. It depends on how much free time I have. If there's a long stretch, I'd really like to write another novel; if not, I'll keep on with short- and mid-form stuff. I don't think I'm the "bellwether"—the community of sci-fi writers in China doesn't qualify as a flock yet, and each of its few sheep has its own distinctive, irreplaceable characteristics. No real bellwether has come to emerge yet, in the market or in literary terms. All we can do is pray that they show up soon.

WE'RE
SCI-FI
FANS

TRANSLATED BY ADAM LANPHIER

Written November 10, 2001, at Niangzi Pass
First published in *Multi-Dimensional Space*, 2002, no. 3

We're mysterious aliens in the crowd. We jump like fleas from future to past and back again, and float like clouds of gas between nebulae; in a flash, we can reach the edge of the universe, or tunnel into a quark, or swim within a star-core . . . We're now as weak and unassuming as fireflies, yet our numbers are growing like grass in spring.

Chinese sci-fi has peaked twice, once in the 1950s and again in the eighties. But no clear boundary then existed between sci-fi and mainstream literature, so no legitimate fan base formed around the genre. After sci-fi came under siege in China in the eighties,* it was abandoned by science and literature alike and left for dead. Then, in an incredible turn, a sci-fi fan base quietly emerged in China. We gave shelter to that half-dead outcast and kept it alive. It went on to sever its umbilical cord to literature and science, establishing an independent identity for itself. This happened in the early nineties, when sci-fi fans were still few and far between.

The third bloom of Chinese sci-fi is currently underway, and though our fan base has expanded dramatically, we're still much smaller than other, comparable communities. *Science Fiction World*, which most of us read, sells between four and five hundred thousand copies each month, which are read by somewhere between one and fifteen million people. Excluding casual readers, we can put the total number of sci-fi fans in China somewhere in the range of five to eight hundred thousand people. This figure includes its share of senior citizens, but secondary school and university students make up its vast majority.

We scrupulously follow the Chinese sci-fi endeavor and hope for it to thrive and achieve liftoff. Many of us read each new story as soon as it's published, regardless of its quality, as if we were duty-bound to do so. Such a phenomenon is rare for other forms of literature. In this

....

* In the late seventies and early eighties, a number of prominent scientists and writers of popular science in China wrote public statements denouncing sci-fi—for its fantasy, in particular, which they deemed "bourgeois." This culminated in an article in *People's Daily* that decried the genre as "spiritual pollution."

regard, we're a lot like China's soccer fans—except they seldom kick a ball themselves, whereas most sci-fi fans, at a certain point, feel compelled to write stories of their own. Very few of us are lucky enough to have our work published; we post most of our stuff online. In dim internet cafés, we type word after word of our very own works of sci-fi, some of which are as long as *War and Peace*. We're the bards errant of the electronic era.

But what's truly essential about our group is this: To us, sci-fi is not merely a genre of literature, but a cohesive world of the spirit—a way of life. We're an advance party, a team of explorers; we travel ahead of others to all manner of future worlds, some foreseeable, others far beyond humanity's potential. We begin with what's real, and from there, our experience radiates outward to every possibility. We're a lot like Alice, there at that convoluted fork in the road: She asks the Cheshire Cat which road to take, and he asks her where she wants to go.

I don't know, she says.

Then it doesn't matter.

Twenty years before all the hype around cloning technology, we'd already tracked down twenty-four young Adolf Hitlers in the world of sci-fi. Now, the sort of life that interests us exists in the form of force fields and light. And it was as many years before nanotechnology entered popular consciousness that a nanosubmarine in sci-fi took its fantastic voyage through the veins of the human body. Now, we're occupied with whether each fundamental particle is its own universe, replete with trillions of galaxies—or whether our universe itself is a fundamental particle. When we're at a newsstand, deciding whether to spend our five yuan on breakfast or a copy of *Science Fiction World*, our spirit has gone to a world of infinite abundance, where each household has a planet of its own. When we're cramming for our final exam, our other self in the spiritual world is on a hundred-billion-light-year expedition into the deep end of the universe. The spiritual world of sci-fi fans is not that of scientists, whose feelers stop far short of where we go. Neither is it that of philosophers, whose world is much less vivid and dynamic than ours. And less still is it the world of myth, as everything in the spiritual world of sci-fi fans might someday come to pass—if it hasn't already, somewhere out there in the far reaches of the universe.

Other people, they don't care for us aliens. When one of us graduates and enters society, we find ourselves surrounded at once by foreign gazes. In this increasingly practical world, lovers of fantasy inspire intense loathing in others. We're forced to hide ourselves deep inside shells of normalcy.

This group of ours may be weak today, but whoever underestimates it is taking their life in their hands. These kids and teenagers are growing up fast. Already, there are Ph.D.s from Beijing and Tsinghua Universities in our midst. More importantly, ours are the most vivacious intellects in society. Ideas that might blow a normal person's mind are nothing but insipid old clichés to us. No one is better prepared than we for the shocking concepts the future holds. We stand far off in the distance and wait impatiently for the world to catch up—and we'll create more astonishing things yet, things that will shake the world.

We sci-fi fans are people from the future.

1967: Ye Wenjie witnesses Red Guards beat her father to death during China's Cultural Revolution. This singular event will shape not only the rest of her life, but also the future of mankind.

Four decades later, Beijing police ask nanotech engineer Wang Miao to infiltrate a secretive cabal of scientists after a spate of inexplicable suicides. Wang's investigation will lead him to a mysterious online game and immerse him in a virtual world ruled by the intractable and unpredictable interaction of its three suns.

This is the Three-Body Problem, and it's the key to everything: the key to the scientists' death, the key to conspiracy that spans light-years, and the key to the extinction-level threat humanity now faces.

Imagine the universe as a forest, patrolled by numberless and nameless predators. In this forest, stealth is survival—any civilization that reveals its location is prey.

Earth has. Now the predators are coming.

Crossing light years, they will reach Earth in four centuries' time. But the sophons, their extra-dimensional agents and saboteurs, are already here. Only the individual human mind remains immune to their influence.

This is the motivation for the Wallfacer Project, a last-ditch defense that grants four individuals almost absolute power to design secret strategies, hidden through deceit and misdirection from human and alien alike. Three of the Wallfacers are influential statesmen and scientists, but the fourth is a total unknown.

Luo Ji, an unambitious Chinese astronomer, is baffled by his new status. All he knows is that he's the one Wallfacer that Trisolaris wants dead.

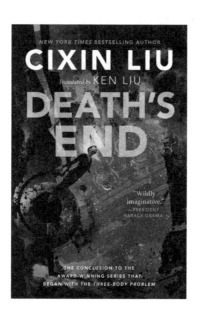

Half a century after the Doomsday Battle, the uneasy balance of Dark Forest Deterrence keeps the Trisolaran invaders at bay.

Earth enjoys unprecedented prosperity due to the infusion of Trisolaran knowledge and, with human science advancing and the Trisolarans adopting Earth culture, it seems that the two civilizations can coexist peacefully as equals without the terrible threat of mutually assured annihilation. But peace has made humanity complacent.

Cheng Xin, an aerospace engineer from the twenty-first century, awakens from hibernation in this new age. She brings knowledge of a long-forgotten program dating from the start of the Trisolar Crisis, and her presence may upset the delicate balance between two worlds. Will humanity reach for the stars or die in its cradle?